"WE'RE GOING TO FIND OUT MORE, AND THEN WE'RE GOING TO FIGHT!

It was enough to curdle the blood. Haendl was proposing to fight—against the invulnerable, the almost godlike Pyramids!

Haendl stood up. "Tropile, that's what this is all about!" He gestured around him. "Guns, tanks, airplanes—it's going to be us against them. Never mind the Sheep; they don't count. It's going to be Pyramids and Wolves, and the Pyramids won't win. And then—"

He was glowing, and the fever was contagious. Tropile felt his own blood begin to pound. Haendl hadn't finished his "and then—", but he didn't have to. It was obvious. And then the Earth would go back to its own solar system, and an end to the five-year cycle of frost and hunger.

And then the Wolves would rule a world worth ruling.

WOLFBANE

FREDERIK POHL

AND

C.M. KORNBLUTH

BAEN
SCIENCE FICTION
BOOKS

WOLFBANE

Copyright © 1986 by Frederik Pohl and C.M. Kornbluth

An earlier and substantially different version of this work was
published under the same title © 1959 by Ballantine Books.

A Baen Books Original

Baen Publishing Enterprises
260 Fifth Avenue
New York, N.Y. 10001

First printing, June 1986

ISBN: 0-671-65576-0

Cover art by Jael

Printed in the United States of America

Distributed by
SIMON & SCHUSTER
TRADE PUBLISHING GROUP
1230 Avenue of the Americas
New York, N.Y. 10020

1

Roget Germyn, banker, of Wheeling, West Virginia, a Citizen, woke gently from a Citizen's dreamless sleep. It was the third-hour-rising time, the time proper to a day of exceptional opportunity to appreciate.

Citizen Germyn dressed himself in the clothes proper for the appreciation of great works—such as viewing the Empire State ruins against stormclouds from a small boat; or walking in silent single file across the remaining course of the Golden Gate Bridge. Or—as today; one hoped that it would be today—witnessing the re-creation of the Sun.

Germyn with difficulty retained a Citizen's necessary calm. When the rekindling of the Sun was late one was tempted to meditate on improper things: would the Sun in fact be re-created? What if it were not? He put his mind to his dress. First of all he put on an old and storied bracelet, a veritable identity brace-

1

let of heavy silver links and a plate which was inscribed:

PFC JOE HARTMANN
Korea 1953

His fellow jewelry-appreciators would have envied him that bracelet—if they had been capable of such an emotion as envy. No other ID bracelet as much as two hundred and fifty years old was known to exist in Wheeling. His finest shirt and pair of light pants went next to his skin, and over them he wore a loose parka whose seams had been carefully weakened. When the Sun was re-created, every five clock-years or so, it was the custom to remove the parka gravely and rend it with the prescribed graceful gestures . . . but not so drastically that it could not be stitched together again. Hence the weakened seams. This was, he counted, the forty-first day on which he and all of Wheeling had donned the appropriate Sun-re-creation clothing. It was the forty-first day on which the Sun—no longer white, no longer blazing yellow, no longer even bright red—had risen and displayed a color that was darker maroon and always darker.

It had, thought Citizen Germyn, never grown so dark and so cold in all of his life. Perhaps it was an occasion for special viewing? For surely it would never come again, this opportunity to see the old Sun so near to death. . . .

One hoped.

Gravely Citizen Germyn completed his dressing, carefully thinking only of the act of dressing itself. Apparel-donning was by no means his specialty, but he considered when it was done that he had done it well, in the traditional flowing gestures, with no flailing, at all times balanced lightly on the ball of the foot. It was all the more perfectly consummated in that no one saw it but himself.

He woke his wife gently, by placing the palm of his hand on her forehead as she lay neatly, in the prescribed fashion, on the Woman's Third of the bed.

The warmth of his hand gradually penetrated her layers of sleep; her eyes demurely opened.

"Citizeness Germyn," he greeted her, making the assurance-of-identity sign with his left hand.

"Citizen Germyn," she said, with the assurance-of-identity inclination of the head which was prescribed when the hands are covered.

He retired to his tiny study to wait.

It was the time appropriate to meditation on the properties of connectivity. Citizen Germyn was skilled in meditation, even for a banker; it was a grace in which he had schooled himself since earliest childhood.

Citizen Germyn, his young face composed, his slim body erect as he sat, but in no way tense or straining, successfully blanked out, one after another, all of the external sounds and sights and feelings that interfered with proper meditation. His mind was very nearly vacant except of one central problem: Connectivity.

Over his head and behind, out of sight, the cold air of the room seemed to thicken and form a blob; a blob of air.

There was a name for those blobs of air; they had been seen before; they were a known fact of existence in Wheeling and in all the world. They were recognized as something associated with meditation on connectivity. They came. They hovered. Then they went away . . . and often did not go away alone.

If someone had been in the room with Citizen Germyn to look at it, he would have seen a distortion, a twisting of what was behind the blob, like flawed glass, a lens; like an eye. And they were called Eye.

Germyn meditated . . .

The blob of air grew and slowly moved. A vagrant current that spun out from it caught a fragment of paper and whirled it to the floor; Germyn stirred; the blob retreated as his meditation, for a moment, was disturbed.

Germyn, all unaware, disciplined his thoughts to disregard the interruption, to return to the central problem of connectivity. The blob hovered . . .

From the other room, his wife's small, thrice-repeated throat-clearing signaled to him that she was decently dressed. Germyn got up to go to her, his mind returning to the world.

Meditation, for that time, was over.

The Eye overhead spun restlessly for a moment. It moved back and forth indecisively, as a man might pace along a train platform when someone with whom he expected to share a journey did not show up.

Then it disappeared.

Some miles east of Wheeling, Glenn Tropile, a Jack of every trade who secretly wondered whether he was a human being, awoke on the couch of his apartment.

He sat up, shivering. It was cold. Damned cold. The damned sun was still damned bloody dark outside the window, and the apartment was soggy and chilled.

He had kicked off the blankets in his sleep— *why* couldn't he learn to sleep quietly, like anybody else? Lacking a robe, he clutched them around him, got up and walked to the unglassed window.

It was not unusual for Glenn Tropile to wake up on his couch. This happened because Gala Tropile had a temper and was inclined to exile him from her bed after a quarrel. He knew he always had the advantage over her for the whole day following the night's exile. Therefore the quarrel was worth it. An advantage was, by definition, worth anything you paid for it . . . or else it was no advantage.

He could hear her moving about in one of the other rooms and cocked an ear, satisfied. She hadn't waked him. Therefore she was about to make amends. A little itch in his spine or his brain—it was not a physical itch, so he couldn't locate it; he could only be sure that it was there—stopped troubling him momentarily; he was winning a contest. It was Glenn Tropile's nature to win contests, and his nature to create them.

Gala Tropile, young, dark, attractive, with a haunted look, came in tentatively carrying coffee from some secret hoard of hers.

Glenn Tropile affected not to notice. He stared coldly out at the cold landscape. The sea, white with thin ice, was nearly out of sight, so far had it retreated as the little sun waned and the spreading polar ice caps hoarded more and more of the water of the seas.

"Glenn—"

Ah, good! *Glenn.* Where was the proper mode of first-greeting-one's-husband? Where was the prescribed throat-clearing upon entering a room? Assiduously he had untaught her the meticulous ritual of manners that they had all of them been brought up to know; and it was the greatest of his many victories over her that sometimes, now, *she* was the aggressor, *she* would be the first to depart from the formal behavior prescribed for Citizens. Depravity! Perversion! Sometimes they would touch each other at times which were not the appropriate coming-together times, Gala sitting on her husband's lap in the late evening, perhaps, or Tropile kissing her awake in the morning. Sometimes he would force her to let him watch her dress—no, not now, for the cold of the waning sun made that sort of frolic unattractive; but she had permitted it before; and such was his mastery over her that he

knew she would permit it again, when the Sun
was re-created. . . .

If, a thought came to him, *if* the Sun was
re-created.

He turned away from the cold outside and
looked at his wife.

"Good morning, darling." She was contrite.

He demanded jarringly: "Is it?" Deliberately he stretched, deliberately he yawned,
deliberately he scratched his chest. Every
movement was ugly. Gala Tropile quivered
but said nothing.

Tropile flung himself on the better of the
two chairs, one hairy leg protruding from under the wrapped blankets. His wife was on her
best behavior—in his unique terms; she didn't
avert her eyes. "What've you got there?" he
asked. "Coffee?"

"Yes, dear. I thought—"

"Where'd you get it?"

The haunted eyes looked away. Good again,
thought Glenn Tropile, more satisfied even
than usual; she's been ransacking an old ware-
house again. It was a trick he had taught her,
and like all of the illicit tricks she had learned
from him a handy weapon when he chose to
use it. It was not prescribed that a Citizeness
should rummage through Old Places. A Citizen did his work, whatever that work might
be—banker, baker or furniture repairman. He
received what rewards were his due for the
work he did. A Citizen *never* took anything
that was not his—no, not even if it lay abandoned and fated to spoil.

It was one of the differences between Glenn Tropile and the people he moved among.

I've got it now, he exulted; it was what he needed to clinch his victory over her. He spoke: "I need you more than I need coffee, Gala."

She looked up, troubled. "What would I do," he demanded, "if a beam fell on you one day while you were scrambling through the fancy groceries? How can you take such chances? Don't you *know* what you mean to me?"

She sniffed a couple of times. She said brokenly: "Darling, about last night—I'm sorry—" and miserably held out the cup. He took it and swallowed the coffee thoughtfully. Then he set it down. He took her hand, looked up at her, and kissed the hand lingeringly.

He felt her tremble. Then she gave him a wild, adoring look and flung herself into his arms.

A new dominance cycle was begun at the moment he returned her frantic kisses.

Glenn knew, and Gala knew, that he had over her an edge—an advantage; the weather gauge; initiative of fire; percentage; the can't-lose vigorish. Call it anything, but it was life itself to Glenn Tropile's kind. He knew, and she knew, that having the advantage he would press it and she would yield—on and on, in a rising spiral. He did it because it was his life, the attaining of an advantage over whomever he might encounter; because he was a Son of the Wolf.

*   *   *

A world away a Pyramid squatted sullenly on the planed-off top of the highest peak of the Himalayas.

It had not been built there. It had not been carried there by man or man's machines. It had come in its own time for its own reasons.

Did it wake on that day, the thing atop Mount Everest? For that matter, did it ever sleep? Nobody knew. It stood or sat, there, approximately a tetrahedron. Its appearance was known; constructed on a base line of some thirty-five yards, slaggy, midnight-blue in color. Human beings had toiled up Everest's grim slopes to learn that much. Almost nothing else about it was known to mankind.

It was the only one of its kind on Earth; though men thought (without much sure knowledge) that there were more, perhaps many more, like it on the unfamiliar planet that was now Earth's binary, swinging around the miniature Sun that now hung at their common center of gravity. But men knew very little about that planet itself, for that matter, only that it had come out of space, and was now there.

Time was when men had tried to give a name to that binary, more than two centuries before, when it first appeared. "Runaway Planet." "The Invader." "Rejoice in Messias, the Day Is at Hand." The labels might as well have been belches; they were sensefree; they were x's in an equation, signifying only that there was *something* there which was unknown.

"The Runaway Planet" stopped running when it closed on Earth.

"The Invader" didn't invade; it merely sent down one slaggy, midnight-blue tetrahedron to Everest.

And "Rejoice in Messias" stole Earth from its sun—with Earth's old moon, which it converted into a miniature sun of its own.

That was the time when men were plentiful and strong—or thought they were; with many huge cities and countless powerful machines. It didn't matter. The new binary planet showed no interest in the cities or the machines. They didn't show any interest in Earth's weapons, either—no, not even when the worst and most deadly of them were deployed against the invaders. The invaders simply went about their business.

Whatever that was.

For four billion years and more the Earth had rolled decorously around the Sun, always in its proper place between the orbits of Venus and Mars, always with its captive Moon for a companion. There was no reason that should ever change.

It did change, though. Something reached out from the interloper planet and changed everything. That something, whatever it was, took hold of the Earth as it sailed around the Sun, and the Earth left its ancient round and followed after, Moon and all. At first the motion was very slow. Then it quickened.

In a week astronomers knew something was happening. In a month the old Sun was perceptibly farther away, tinier, less warming. There was panic about that—added to all the other panics that swept the globe.

Then the Moon sprang into flame.

That was a problem in nomenclature, too. What do you call a Moon when it becomes a Sun? It did, though. Just in time, for already the parent Sol was visibly more distant, and in a few years it was only one other star among many.

When the inferior little sun was burned to a clinker *they*—whoever "they" were, for men saw only the one Pyramid—would hang a new one in the sky; it happened every five clock-years, more or less. It was the same old moon-turned-sun; but it burned out, and the fires needed to be rekindled. The first of these suns had looked down on an Earthly population of ten billion. As the sequence of suns waxed and waned there were changes; climatic fluctuation; all but immeasurable differences in the quantity and kind of radiation from the new source.

The changes were such that the forty-fifth such sun looked down on a shrinking human race that could not muster up a hundred million.

A frustrated man drives inward; it is the same with a race. The hundred million that clung to existence were not the same as the bold, vital ten billion.

The thing on Everest had in its time re-ceived many labels, too: The Devil, The Friend,

The Beast, A Pseudo-living Entity of Quite Unknown Electrochemical Properties.

All these labels were also x's.

If it did wake that morning it did not open its eyes, for it had no eyes—apart from the quivers of air that might or might not belong to it. Eyes might have been gouged; therefore it had none; so an illogical person might have argued—and yet it was tempting, to apply the "purpose, not function" fallacy to it. Limbs could be crushed; it had no limbs. Ears could be deafened; it had none. Through a mouth it might be poisoned; it had no mouth. Intentions and actions could be frustrated; apparently it had neither.

It was there; that was all.

It and others like it had stolen the Earth and the Earth did not know why. It was there. And the one thing on Earth you could not do was hurt it, influence it, or coerce it in any way whatever.

It was there—and it, or the masters it represented, owned the Earth by right of theft. Utterly. Beyond human hope of challenge or redress.

2

Citizen and Citizeness Roget Germyn walked down Pine Street in the chill and dusk of— one hoped—a Sun Re-creation Morning.

It was the convention to pretend that this was a morning like any other morning. It was not proper either to cast frequent hopeful glances at the sky, nor yet to seem disturbed or afraid because this was, after all, the forty-first such morning since those whose specialty was Sky-Viewing had come to believe the Re-creation of the Sun was near.

The Citizen and his Citizeness exchanged the assurance-of-identity sign with a few old friends and stopped to converse. This also was a convention of skill divorced from purpose; the conversation was without relevance to any-thing that any one of the participants might know, or think, or wish to ask. Germyn said for his friends a twenty-word poem he had made in honor of the occasion and heard their responses. They did line-capping for a while until somebody indicated unhappiness and a wish to change by frowning the Two Grooves between his brows. The game was deftly ended with an improvised rhymed exchange.

Casually Citizen Germyn glanced aloft. The sky-change had not begun yet; the dying old Sun hung just over the horizon, east and south, much more south than east. It was an ugly thought, but suppose, thought Germyn, just *suppose* that the Sun were not re-created today? Or tomorrow or—

Or ever.

The Citizen got a grip on himself and told his wife: "We shall dine at the oatmeal stall."

The Citizeness did not immediately reply. When Germyn glanced at her with well-masked surprise he found her almost staring down the dim street, at a Citizen who moved almost in a stride, almost swinging his arms. Scarcely graceful.

"That might be more Wolf than man," she said doubtfully.

Germyn knew the fellow. Tropile was his name. One of those curious few who made their homes outside of Wheeling, though they were not farmers; Germyn had had banker's dealings with him.

"That is a careless man," he said, "and an ill-bred one." They moved toward the oatmeal stall with the gait of Citizens, arms limp, feet scarcely lifted, slumped forward a little. It was the ancient gait of fifteen hundred calories per day, not one of which could be squandered.

There was a need for more calories. So many for walking, so many for gathering food. So many for the economical pleasures of the Citizens, and so many more—oh, many more, these days!—to keep out cold. Yet there were no more calories; the diet the whole world lived on was a bare subsistence ration. It was impossible to farm well when half the world's land was part of the time drowned in the rising sea, part of the time smothered in falling snow. Citizens knew this and, knowing, did not struggle—it was ungraceful to struggle, particularly when one could not win. Only the horrors known as Wolves struggled, splurging calories, reckless of grace.

Wolves! Why must there be Wolves? Why must those few, secret, despicable monsters threaten the whole fabric of civilized behavior?

Of course, Roget Germyn himself had once been a Wolf—at least, a Cub. Everybody started out that way. That was what children were. You began by wailing when you were hungry and taking whatever there was to take. Little kids weren't expected to understand the rules of conduct. Certainly they were not equipped to understand how vital those rules were to survival itself.

Form follows function. The customs of Citizen Germyn's world developed out of urgent need. That tiny Sun, né Moon, produced only enough warmth for marginal survival. There was not enough food to go around. There was not enough of anything to go around; so everyone was carefully schooled, from the age of two onward, to eat sparingly, move slowly, contemplate instead of act. Even what one contemplated was carefully prescribed. It was not wise to daydream about food or new clothes or the pleasures of the marriage bed. Such dreams led to desires. Desires were hard to control. The best things to contemplate were sunsets, storm clouds, stars, the gracefully ser-endipitous trickle of a single raindrop down a windowpane—no one was ever impelled to *desire* a raindrop. Best of all was to meditate on connectivity. When you thought about how everything was connected to everything else— was a part of everything else—*was* everything else, why, then the mind emptied itself. There was no "wanting" when you meditated on connectivity. There was no thinking. There was only being.

A well-brought-up Citizen could spend thousands of hours out of his life in such meditation—hours that were by definition saved from eating, acting, doing, lusting—any of those so very undesirable things.

The things that Wolves did.

One could go even farther. It sometimes happened that a Citizen would attain the ultimate. Non-acting rose to become non-wanting, and then non-thinking . . . and then, perhaps, he would attain the final grace:

Non-being.

When you attained non-being you simply disappeared, with a clap of nearby thunder. And all who were left behind would praise your memory—tepidly, and with dignity.

That was how Citizens should behave. That was how everyone did behave—

Except Wolves.

It was unseemly to think too much of Wolves. It led to anger, which was very wasteful of calories. Citizen Germyn turned his mind to more pleasant things.

He allowed himself his First Foretaste of the oatmeal. It would be warm in the bowl, hot in the throat, a comfort in the stomach. There was a great deal of pleasure there, in weather like this, when the cold plucked through the loosened seams and the wind came up the sides of the hills. Not that there wasn't pleasure in the cold itself, for that matter. It was proper that one should be cold now, just before the re-creation of the Sun, when the old Sun was smoky red and the new one not yet kindled.

"—Still looks like Wolf to me," his wife was muttering.

"Cadence," Germyn reproved his Citizeness, but took the sting out of it with a Quirked Smile. The man with the ugly manners was standing at the very bar of the oatmeal stall where they were heading. In the gloom of mid-morning he was all angles, and strained lines; his head was turned awkwardly on his shoulder, peering toward the back of the stall where the vendor was rhythmically measuring grain into a pot; his hands were resting helter-skelter on the counter, not hanging by his sides.

Citizen Germyn felt a faint shudder from

his wife. But he did not reprove her again, for who could blame her? The exhibition was revolting.

She said faintly, "Citizen, might we dine on bread this morning?"

He hesitated and glanced again at the ugly man. He said indulgently, knowing that he was indulgent: "On Sun Re-creation Morning, the Citizeness may dine on bread." Bearing in mind the occasion, it was only a small favor, and therefore a very proper one.

The bread was good, very good. They shared out the half-kilo between them and ate it in silence, as it deserved. Germyn finished his first portion and, in the prescribed pause before beginning his second, elected to refresh his eyes upward.

He nodded to his wife and stepped outside. Overhead the Old Sun parceled out its last barrel-scrapings of heat. It was larger than the stars around it, but many of them were nearly as bright. There was one star in Earth's sky which was brighter than the dying fire on the old Moon, but it happened to be in the other half of the heavens at this time. When it was visible, people looked at it wistfully. It was the Earth's parent star, receding always behind them.

Germyn shivered slightly in the dusky morning air. Wheeling, West Virginia, was a splendid place to be in the summer, when a New Sun was bright. Harvests were bountiful, the polar caps released their ice and the oceans returned to drown the coastal plains. It was less good to be in these mountains when the Old Sun was dying. It was *cold*.

Cycle after cycle, as each Sun aged, Citizen Germyn and his Citizeness ritually debated the question of whether they should remain in Wheeling or join the more adventurous migrants in their trek to sea level, and the slightly warmer conditions along the coasts. Since they were model Citizens, the decision was always to remain—one wasted fewer calories that way. And of course the New Sun always came just when it was most needed—always had before, at least.

He was saved from pursuing that thought when a high-pitched male voice said: "Citizen Germyn, good morning."

Germyn was caught off balance. He took his eyes off the sky, half-turned, glanced at the face of the person who had spoken to him, raised his hand in the assurance-of-identity sign. It was all very quick and fluid—almost too quick, for he had had his fingers bent nearly into the sign for female friends; and this was a man. Citizen Boyne; Germyn knew him well; they had shared the Ice Viewing at Niagara a year before.

Germyn recovered quickly enough, but it had been disconcerting.

He improvised quickly: "There are stars, but are stars still there if there is no Sun?" It was a hurried effort, he grieved, but no doubt Boyne would pick it up and carry it along; Boyne had always been very good, very graceful.

Boyne did no such thing. "Good morning," he said again, faintly. He glanced at the stars overhead as though trying to unravel what Germyn was talking about. He said accusingly, his voice cracking sharply: "There isn't any Sun, Germyn. What do you think of that?"

Germyn swallowed. "Citizen, perhaps you—"

"No Sun, you hear me!" The man sobbed, "It's cold, Germyn. The Pyramids aren't going to give us another Sun, do you know that? They're going to starve us, freeze us; they're through with us. We're done, all of us!" He was nearly screaming. All up and down Pine Street people were trying not to look at him, some of them failing.

Boyne clutched at Germyn helplessly. Revolted, Germyn drew back—bodily contact!

It seemed to bring the man to his senses. Reason returned to his eyes. He said, "I—" He stopped, stared about him. "I think I'll have bread for breakfast," he said foolishly, and plunged into the stall.

Strained voice, shouting, clutching, no manners at all!

Boyne left behind him a shaken Citizen, caught half-way into the wrist-flip of parting, staring after him with jaw slack and eyes wide, as though Germyn had no manners either.

All this on Sun Re-creation Day!

What could it mean? Germyn wondered fretfully. Was Boyne on the point of— Could Boyne be about to—

He drew back from the thought. There was one thing that might explain Boyne's behavior. But it was not a proper speculation for one Citizen to make about another.

All the same—Germyn dared the thought— all the same, it *did* seem almost as though Citizen Boyne were on the point of, well, running amok.

At the oatmeal stall, Glenn Tropile thumped on the counter.

The laggard oatmeal vendor finally brought the bowl of salt and the pitcher of thin milk. Tropile took his paper twist of salt from the top of the neatly arranged pile in the bowl. He glanced at the vendor; his fingers hesitated; then quickly he ripped the twist of paper into his oatmeal and covered it to the permitted level with the milk.

He ate quickly and efficiently, watching the street outside.

They were wandering and mooning about, as always—maybe today more than most days, since they hoped it would be the day the Sun blossomed flame once more.

Tropile always thought of the wandering, mooning Citizens as *they*. There was a "we" somewhere for Tropile, no doubt, but Tropile had not as yet located it, not even in the bonds of the marriage contract. He was in no hurry. At the age of fourteen Glenn Tropile had reluctantly come to realize certain things about himself; that he disliked being bested; that he had to have a certain advantage in all his dealings, or an intolerable itch of the mind drove him to discomfort. The things added up to a terrifying fear, gradually becoming knowledge, that the only "we" that could properly include him was one that it was not very wise to join.

He had realized, in fact, that he was a Wolf.

For some years Tropile had struggled against it—for Wolf was a bad word, the children he played with were punished severely for saying it, and for almost nothing else. It was not *proper* for one Citizen to advantage himself at the expense of another; Wolves did that. It was *proper* for a Citizen to accept what he had, not to strive for more; to find beauty in small things; to accommodate himself, with the minimum of strain and awkwardness, to whatever his life happened to be. Wolves were not like that; Wolves never Meditated, Wolves never Appreciated, Wolves *never* were Translated. That supreme fulfillment, granted only to those who succeeded in a perfect meditation on connectivity—that surrender of the world and the flesh by taking leave of both— that could never be achieved by a Wolf.

Accordingly, Glenn Tropile had tried very hard to do all the things that Wolves could not do.

He had nearly succeeded; his specialty, Water Watching, had been most rewarding; he had achieved many partly successful meditations on connectivity.

And yet he was still a Wolf; for he still felt that burning, itching urge to triumph and to hold an advantage. For that reason, it was almost impossible for him to make friends among the Citizens and gradually he had almost stopped trying.

Tropile had arrived in Wheeling nearly a year before, making him one of the early settlers in point of time. And yet there was not a Citizen in the street who was prepared to exchange recognition gestures with him.

He knew *them*, nearly every one. He knew their names and their wives' names; he knew what northern states they had moved down from with the spreading of the ice, as the sun grew dim; he knew very nearly to the quarter of a gram what stores of sugar and salt and coffee each one of them had put away—for their guests, of course, not for themselves; the well-bred Citizen hoarded only for the entertainment of others. He knew these things because there was an advantage to Tropile in knowing them. But there was no advantage in having anyone know him.

A few did—that banker, Germyn; for Tropile had approached him only a few months before about a prospective loan. But it had been a chancy, nervous encounter; the idea was so luminously simple to Tropile—organize an expedition to the coal mines that once had flourished nearby; find the coal, bring it to Wheeling, heat the houses. And yet it had sounded blasphemous to Germyn. Tropile had counted himself lucky merely to have been refused the loan, instead of being cried out upon as Wolf.

*   *   *

The oatmeal vendor was fussing worriedly around his neat stack of paper twists in the salt bowl.

Tropile avoided the man's eyes. Tropile was not interested in the little wry smile of self-deprecation which the vendor would make to him, given half a chance; Tropile knew well enough what was disturbing the vendor. Let it disturb him. It was Tropile's custom to take extra twists of salt; they were in his pockets now; they would stay there. Let the vendor wonder why he was short.

Tropile licked the bowl of his spoon and stepped into the street. He was comfortably aware under a double-thick parka that the wind was blowing very cold.

A Citizen passed him, walking alone: odd, thought Tropile. He was walking rapidly, and there was a look of taut despair on his face. Still more odd. Odd enough to be worth another look, because that sort of haste, that sort of abstraction, suggested something to Tropile. They were in no way normal to the gentle sheep of the class *They*, except in one particular circumstance.

Glenn Tropile crossed the street to follow the abstracted Citizen, whose name, he knew, was Boyne. The man blundered into Citizen Germyn outside the baker's stall, and Tropile stood back out of easy sight, watching and listening.

Boyne was on the ragged edge of breakdown. What Tropile heard and saw confirmed his diagnosis. The one particular circumstance was close to happening; Citizen Boyne was on the verge of a total lack of control. The circumstances had a name, borrowed from the language of a now uninhabited Pacific island where simple farmers, pushed too far, would turn rogue, slashing and killing with their cane-cutting knives.

It was called "running amok."

Tropile looked at the man with amusement and contempt. Amok! The gentle sheep could be pushed too far, after all! He had seen it before; the signs were obvious.

There was sure to be an advantage in it for Glenn Tropile; there was an advantage in anything, if you looked for it. He watched and waited. He picked his spot with care, so that he could see Citizen Boyne inside the baker's stall, making a dismal botch of slashing his quarter-kilo of bread from the Morning Loaf.

He waited for Boyne to come racing out . . .

Boyne did.

A yell—loud, piercing: It was Citizen Germyn, shrilling: "Amok, amok!" A scream. An enraged wordless cry from Boyne, and the baker's knife glinting in the faint light as Boyne swung it. And then Citizens were scattering in every direction—all of the Citizens but one.

One citizen was under the knife—his own knife, as it happened; it was the baker himself. Boyne chopped and chopped again. And then Boyne came out, like a roaring flame, the bread knife whistling about his head. The gentle Citizens fled panicked before him. He struck at their retreating forms, and screamed and struck again. Amok!

It was the one particular circumstance when they forgot to be gracious—one of the two, Tropile corrected himself as he strolled across to the baker's stall. His brow furrowed; because there was another circumstance when they lacked grace, and one which affected him more nearly.

He watched the maddened creature, Boyne, already far down the road, chasing a knot of Citizens around a corner. Tropile sighed and stepped into the baker's stall to see what he might gain from this. Boyne would wear himself out; the surging **rage** would leave him as quickly as it came; he would be a sheep again, and the other sheep would close in and capture him. That was what happened when a Citizen ran amok. It was a measure of what pressures were on the Citizens that at any moment there might be one gram of pressure too much, and one of them would crack. It happened all the time. It had happened here in Wheeling twice within the past two months; Glenn Tropile had seen it happen in Pittsburgh, Altoona and Bronxville.

There is a limit to pressure.

Tropile walked into the baker's stall and looked down without emotion at the slaughtered baker; Tropile had seen corpses before.

He looked around the stall, calculating. As a starter, he bent to pick up the quarter-kilo of bread Boyne had dropped, dusted it off and slipped it into his pocket. Food was always useful. Given enough food, perhaps Boyne would not have run amok. Was it simple hunger they cracked under? Or the knowledge of the thing on Mount Everest, or the hovering Eyes, or the sought-after-dreaded prospect of Translation, or merely the strain of keeping up their laboriously figured lives? Did it matter? *They* cracked and ran amok, and Tropile never would, and that was what mattered.

He leaned across the counter, reaching for what was left of the Morning Loaf—

And found himself staring into the terrified large eyes of Citizeness Germyn.

She screamed: "Wolf! Citizens, help me! Here is a Wolf!"

Tropile faltered. He hadn't even *seen* the damned woman, but there she was, rising up from behind the counter, screaming her head off: "Wolf, Wolf!"

He said sharply: "Citizeness, I beg you—" But that was no good. The evidence was on him, and her screams would fetch others. Tropile panicked. He started toward her to silence her; but that was no good, either. He whirled. She was screaming, screaming, and there were people to hear. Tropile darted into the street, but they were popping out of every doorway now, they were appearing from each rat's hole in which they had hid to escape Boyne. "Please!" he cried, angry and frightened. "Wait a minute!" But they weren't waiting. They had heard the woman, and maybe some of them had seen him with the bread. They were all around him—no, they were all over him; they were clutching at him, tearing at his soft, warm furs. They pulled at his pockets, and the stolen twists of salt spilled accusingly out. They ripped at his sleeves, and even the stout, unweakened seams ripped open. He was fairly captured.

"Wolf!" they were shouting. "Wolf!" It drowned out the distant noise from where Boyne had finally been run to earth, a block and more away. It drowned out everything.

It was the other circumstance when *they* forgot to be gracious: When they had trapped a Son of the Wolf.

3

Engineering had long ago come to an end.

Engineering is possible under one condition of the equation:

$$\frac{Total\ Available\ Calories}{Population.} = \text{Artistic-Technological Style}$$

When the ratio Calories-to-Population is large—say five thousand or more, five thousand daily calories for every living man—then the Artistic-Technological Style is *big*. People carve Mount Rushmore; they build great foundries; they manufacture an enormous automobile to carry one housewife half a mile for the purchase of one lipstick. Life is coarse and rich where C:P is large. At the other extreme, where C:P is too small, life does not exist at all. It has been starved out.

Experimentally, add little increments to C:P and it will be some time before the right-hand side of the equation becomes significant. But at last, in the 1,000–1,500 calorie range, Artistic-

Technological Style firmly appears in self-perpetuating form. C:P in that range produces the small arts, the appreciations, the peaceful arrangements of necessities into subtle relationships of traditionally-agreed-upon virtue. Japan, locked into its Shogunate prison, picked scanty food from mountainsides and beauty out of arrangements of lichens and paper. The small, inexpensive sub-sub-arts are characteristic of the 1,000–1,500 calorie range.

And this was the range of Earth; the world of a hundred million men, after the planet was stolen by its new binary.

Some few persons inexpensively pursued the study of science with pencil and renewable paper, but the last research accelerator had long since been shut down; the juice from its hydropower dam was needed to supply meager light to a million homes and to cook the pablum for two million brand-new babies. In those days, one dedicated Byzantine wrote the definitive encyclopedia of engineering (though he was no engineer). Its four hundred and twenty tiny volumes exhausted the Gizeh pyramid and its unknown contractor, the Wall of Shih-Hwang Ti, the Gothic builders, Brunel who changed the face of England, the Roeblings of Brooklyn, Groves of the Pentagon, Duggan of the Anti-Ballistic-Missile System (before C:P dropped to the point where war became vanishingly implausible), Levern of Operation Up. But this encyclopedist could not use a slide rule without thinking, faltering, jotting down his decimals.

And then the magnitudes grew less.

Under the tectonic and climatic battering of the great abduction of Earth from its primary, under the sine-wave advances to and retreats from the equator of the ice sheath as the small successor Suns waxed, waned, died and were replaced, the ratio C:P remained stable. C had diminished enormously; so had P. As the calories to support life grew scarce, so the consuming mouths of mankind grew fewer in number.

The forty-fifth small Sun shone on no engineers.

Not even on the binary. The Pyramids, the things on the binary, the thing on Mount Everest, were not engineers. They employed a crude metaphysic based on dissection and shoving.

They had no elegant field theories. All they knew was that everything came apart and that if you pushed a thing it would move. If your biggest push would not move a thing, you took it apart and pushed the parts, and then it would move. Sometimes, for nuclear effects, they had to take things apart into as many as 3×10^9 pieces, and shove each piece very carefully.

By taking-apart and shoving, then, they landed their one space ship on the burnt-out sunlet that had once been Earth's familiar Moon. You could not say that the Pyramids were late in the re-creation of the Sun. The Pyramids were never late. That was impossible to them, for they had no sense of time at all. They knew "when" things must be done, because they possessed a planet-sized network of instruments, actuators and ancillary devices of every sort. When the mean global temperature of the Earth dropped below a certain pre-set value, a sensor reported the need to rekindle the Moon. Then it was done. The pyramids did not concern themselves with fiddly little details such as the movement of Earth's air masses. It happened that Australia and Africa were exceptionally balmy that year, so the global average was slow to drop . . . and the calculations of the Skywatchers therefore wrong.

But now it was "time" and the space ship was sent out.

Inside it were eleven men and women, along with a few other, very different living things.

These were not exactly passengers. "Fittings" was a better word. Since they had long since lost any awareness of language, or even of self, words did not concern them.

Centuries ago, other human beings had lalumphed across the Moon in clumsy space-suits, radioing congratulatory messages back to Earth like happy tourists. In the two hundred years and more since human beings had last been able to get into space under their own power, many hundreds of humans (and others) had visited the satellite. None of those had been tourists, either. They had done just what the present batch did.

They restarted the nuclear fires which turned the Moon into an almost-star. To do this was quite difficult, even with the machines and instruments that had accompanied them from the binary planet. Among other things, it was necessary for them to die.

Even for the instruments of the Pyramids, kindling a nuclear fire on the surface of the Moon was not easy. There was really nothing there to burn. The Moon was made out of rock and dust—and now of slag as well; its elements were not the kind that would readily fission or fuse. But when the devices of the Pyramids had sufficiently taken-apart-and-shoved, neutrons crowded protons out of cores, nuclei crumbled, energy was released. Enough energy so that the new Sun would burn for five years or so before it needed relighting.

So the space ship touched down, briefly, on a hillock on the Moon that was no longer burning, but only intolerably hot.

The space ship deposited a detachable capsule containing the eleven human beings (and others) and the necessary machinery for taking apart and shoving. Then the space ship quickly departed, to avoid what would follow.

Where the capsule touched the hot slag, heat flowed in. The human beings did not notice. They were only aware that their tasks must be performed very quickly now.

They performed them, racing against the mounting heat that would soon cook them to a point where they could no longer function; and the New Sun was re-created.

A point of new flame appeared on the sunlet's surface. The eleven human beings had time to scream briefly before they died. Then the point of flame went from cherry through orange into blue-white, and began to spread.

At the moment of the Re-Creation of the Sun there was general rejoicing on the Earth. Wherever people survived, in shadowy remnants of cities called Khartoum and Chicago and Beijing, the Citizens smiled with controlled joy at the sky.

Not quite everywhere, though. In Wheeling's House of the Five Regulations, Glenn Tropile waited unquietly for death. Citizen Boyne, who had run amok and slaughtered the baker, shared Tropile's room and his doom, but not his rage. Boyne with demure pleasure was composing his death poem.

"Talk to me!" snapped Tropile. "Why are we here? What did you do, and why did you do it? What have I done? Why don't I pick up a bench and kill you with it? You would've killed me two hours ago if I'd caught your eye!"

There was no satisfaction in Citizen Boyne. The passions were burned out of him; he politely tendered Trophile a famous aphorism: "Citizen, the art of living is the substitution of unimportant, answerable questions for important, unanswerable ones. Come, let us appreciate the new-born Sun."

He turned to the window, where the spark of blue-white flame in what had once been the

crater of Tycho was beginning to spread across
the charred moon.

Tropile was child enough of his culture to
turn with him almost involuntarily. He was
silent. That blue-white infinitesimal up there
growing slowly—the one-ness, the calm rapture of Being in a universe that you shaded
into without harsh discontinua, the being one
with the great blue-white gem-flower blossom-
ing now in the heavens that were no different
stuff than you yourself—

He closed his eyes, calm, and meditated on
connectivity.

He was being Good.

By the time the fusion reaction had covered
the whole small disk of the sunlet, a quarter-
hour at the most, his meditation began to
wear off, as it generally did for Glenn Tropile.
That was good, he thought, as it seemed to
exempt him from the worrisome possibility of
Translation. He had no desire simply one day
to disappear.

All the same, he sometimes felt just a touch
of regret.

Tropile shrugged out of his torn parka, not
bothering to rip it further. It was already growing warm in the room. Citizen Boyne, of course,
was carefully opening every seam with graceful rending motions, miming great smooth effort of the biceps and trapezius.

But the meditation was over, and as Tropile
watched his cellmate he screamed a silent *Why?*
Since his adolescence that wailing syllable had

seldom been far from his mind. It could be silenced by appreciation and meditation. Tropile was so good at his specialty of Water Watching that several beginners had asked him for instruction in the subtle art, for all his notorious oddities of life and manner. He *enjoyed* Water Watching. He almost pitied anybody so single-mindedly devoted to, say, Clouds and Odors—great games though they were—that he had never even tried Water Watching. And after a session of Watching, when one was lucky enough to observe the Nine Boiling Stages in classic perfection, one might slip into meditation and be harmonious, feel Good.

But what did one do when the meditations failed—as they had failed him? What did one do when they came farther and farther apart, became less and less intense, could be inspired, finally, only by a huge event like the renewal of the Sun?

One went amok, he had always thought.

But he had not; Boyne had. He had been declared a Son of the Wolf, on no evidence that he could understand. But he had not run amok.

Still the penalties were the same, he thought, uncomfortably aware of an unfamiliar itch—not the inward intolerable itch of needing-the-advantage, but a realized sensation at the base of his spine. The penalties for all gross crimes— Wolfhood or running amok—were the same, and simply this: They would perform the Lumbar Puncture. He would make the Donation of Fluid.

He would be dead.

The Keeper of the House of the Five Regulations, an old man, Citizen Harmane, looked in on his charges—approvingly at Boyne, with a beclouded expression at Glenn Tropile. It was thought that even Wolves were entitled to the common human decencies in the brief interval between exposure and the Donation of Fluid. The Keeper would not have dreamed of scowling at the detected Wolf or of interfering with whatever wretched imitation of meditation-before-dying the creature might practice. But he could not, all the same, bring himself to offer even an assurance-of-identity gesture.

Tropile had no such qualms.

He scowled at Keeper Harmane with such ferocity that the old man almost ran away. Tropile turned an almost equally ugly scowl upon Citizen Boyne. How dared that knife-murderer be so calm, so relaxed!

Tropile said brutally: "They'll kill us! You know that? They'll stick a needle in our spines and drain us dry. It *hurts*. Do you understand me? They're going to drain us, and then they're going to drink our spinal fluid, and it's going to *hurt*."

He was gently corrected. "We shall make the Donation of fluid, which is proper for Citizens who have grossly misbehaved. That is all," Citizen Boyne said calmly. "Is not the difference intelligible to a Son of the Wolf?"

True culture demanded that that remark be accepted as a friendly joke, probably based on a truth—how else could an unpalatable truth be put in words? Otherwise the unthinkable might happen. They might quarrel. They might even come to blows! A person might be *hurt* that way!

The appropriate mild smile formed on Tropile's lips, but harshly he wiped it off. They were going to stab him in the spine with a great catheter and *kill* him. He would *not* smile for them! And the effort was enormous.

"I'm *not* a Son of the Wolf!" he howled, desperate, knowing he was protesting to the one man of all men in Wheeling who didn't care, and who could do least about it if he did. "What's this crazy talk about Wolves? I don't know what a Son of the Wolf is, and I don't think you or anybody does. All I know is that I was acting *sensibly*. And everybody began howling! You're supposed to know a Son of the Wolf by his unculture, his ignorance, his violence. But you chopped down three people, and I only picked up a piece of bread! And *I'm* supposed to be the dangerous one!"

"Wolves never know they're Wolves," sighed Citizen Boyne. "Fish probably think they're birds, and you evidently think you're a Citizen. Would a Citizen speak as you are speaking?"

"But they're going to kill us!"

"Then why aren't you composing your death poem?"

Glenn Tropile took a deep breath. Something was biting him.

It was bad enough that he was about to die, bad enough that he had done nothing worth dying for. But what was gnawing at him now had nothing to do with dying.

The percentages were going the wrong way. This pale Citizen was getting an edge on him.

An engorged gland in Tropile's adrenals—it was only a pinhead in Citizen Boyne's—trickled subtle hormones into his bloodstream. He could die, yes—that was a skill everyone had to acquire, sooner or later. But while he was alive, he could not stand to be bested in an encounter, an argument, a relationship. It was not in Glenn Tropile's makeup to allow anyone to defeat him, in anything, without a fight. Wolf? Call him Wolf. Call him Operator, or Percentage Player; call him Sharp Article; call him Gamesman.

If there was an advantage to be derived, he would derive it. It was the way he was put together.

He said, stalling for time to scheme, "You're right. Stupid of me, I must have lost my head!"

He thought. Some men think by poking problems apart, some think by laying facts side-by-side to compare. Tropile's thinking was neither of these, but a species of judo. He conceded to his opponent such things as Strength, Armor, Resource. He didn't need these things for himself; to every contest the opponent brought enough of them to supply two. It was Tropile's habit (and definitely a Wolfish one, he had to admit) to use the opponent's strength against him, to break the opponent against his own steel walls.

He thought.

The first thing, he thought, was to make up his mind: He was Wolf. Then let him *be* Wolf; he wouldn't stay around for the spinal tap, he would go from there. But how?

The second thing was to make a plan. There were obstacles. Citizen Boyne was one of the obstacles. Harmane, the Keeper of the House of the Five Regulations, was another.

Where was the pole which would permit him to vault over these hurdles? There was, he thought, always his wife, Gala. He owned her; she would do what he wished—provided he made her *want* to do it.

Yes, Gala. He walked to the door and shouted to Citizen Harmane: "Keeper! Keeper, I must see my wife. Have her brought to me!"

It was impossible for the Keeper to refuse; he didn't. He called gently, "I will invite the Citizeness," and toddled away.

The third thing was time.

Tropile turned to Citizen Boyne. "Citizen," he said persuasively, "since your death poem is ready and mine is not, will you be gracious enough to go first when they—when they come?"

Citizen Boyne looked temperately at his cellmate and made the Quirked Smile.

"You see?" he said. "Wolf." And that was true; but what was also true was that he couldn't refuse.

4

Half a world away, the midnight-blue Pyramid sat on its planed-off peak as it had sat since the days when Earth had a real Sun of its own.

It was of no importance to the Pyramid that Glenn Tropile was about to receive a slim catheter into his spine, to drain his sap and his life. It didn't matter to the Pyramid that the spinal fluid would then be swallowed by his fellows, or that the pretext for the execution was an act which human history used not to consider a capital crime. Ritual sacrifice in whatever guise made no difference to the Pyramid. The Pyramid saw them come and the Pyramid saw them go—if the Pyramid could be said to "see". One human being more or less, what matter? Who bothers to take a census of the cells in a hangnail?

And yet, the Pyramid did have a kind of

interest in Glenn Tropile, and in the human race of which he was a part.

Nobody knew much about the Pyramid, but everybody knew *that* much. They wanted something—else why would they have bothered to steal the Earth?

And that they had definitely done.

The year was 2027 A.D., a true date to live in infamy. There were other years that human beings had chosen to remember—1941; 1066; 1492—but nothing, ever, with consequences so vast as the year 2027, no, not since those earliest and forgotten dates when the first amphibian crawled out of the sea or the first hairy biped picked up a tool. Twenty twenty-seven topped them all. The Runaway Planet had slipped feloniously into the solar system, intent on burglary, and ever since it had been making off with its plunder.

Courageous human beings had blasted out into space to investigate. Three shiploads of them had actually landed on the Pyramid planet (they didn't know that was what it was, then.) They didn't even report, really. The first message back, right after touchdown, was, "It seems, ah, very *barren.*" There wasn't any second.

Perhaps those landings were a mistake. Some thought so. Some thought that if the human race had cowered silent under its blanket of air the Pyramids might have run right through the ecliptic and away.

However, the triumphal "mistake" was made,

and that may have been the first time a human eye saw a Pyramid.

Shortly after—though not before the radio message was sent—that human eye winked out forever; but by then the damage was done. What passed in a Pyramid for "attention" had been attracted. The next thing that happened set the wireless channels between Palomar and Pernambuco, between Greenwich and the Cape of Good Hope, buzzing and worrying, as astronomers all over the Earth reported and confirmed and reconfirmed the astonishing fact that our planet was on the move. *Rejoice in Messias* had come to take us away.

A world of ten billion people, some of them brilliant, many of them brave, built and flung the giant rockets of Operation Up at the invader: Nothing.

The two ships of the Interplanetary Expeditionary Force were boosted up to no-gravity and dropped onto the new planet to strike back: Nothing.

Earth moved spirally outward.

If a battle could not be won, then perhaps a migration. New ships were built in haste. But they lay there rusting as the sun grew small and the ice grew thick; because where was there to go? Not Mars; not the Moon which was trailing along; not choking Venus or crushing Jupiter.

The migration was defeated as surely as the war, there being no place to migrate to.

One Pyramid came to Earth, only one. It shaved the crest off the highest mountain there was, and squatted on it. An observer? A warden? Whatever it was, it stayed.

The Sun grew too distant to be of use, and out of the old Moon the Pyramid-aliens built a new small sun in the sky—a five-year sun, that burned out and was replaced, again and again and endlessly again. It had been a fierce struggle against unbeatable odds on the part of the ten billion; and when the uselessness of struggle was demonstrated at last, many of the ten billion froze to death, and many of them starved, and nearly all of the rest had something frozen or starved out of them; and what was left, two centuries and more later, was more or less like Citizen Boyne, except for a few, a very few, like Glenn Tropile.

Gala Tropile stared miserably at her husband. "—Want to get out of here," he was saying urgently. "They want to kill me. Gala, you know you can't make yourself suffer by letting them kill me!"

She wailed: "I *can't!*"

Tropile looked over his shoulder. Citizen Boyne was fingering the textured contrasts of a golden watch-case which had been his father's—and soon would be his son's. Boyne's eyes were closed and he wasn't listening.

Tropile leaned forward and deliberately put his hand on his wife's arm. She started and flushed, of course; he could feel her trembling.

"You *can*," he said, "and what's more, you will. You can help me get out of here. I insist on it, Gala, because I must save you that pain." He took his hand off her arm, content. He said harshly: "Darling, don't you think I know how much we've always meant to each other?"

She looked at him wretchedly. Fretfully she tore at the billowing filmy sleeve of her summer blouse. The seams hadn't been loosened, there hadn't been time. She had just been getting into the appropriate Sun Re-creation Day costume, to be worn under the parka, when the messenger had come with the news about her husband.

She avoided his eyes. "If you're really Wolf . . ."

Tropile's sub-adrenals pulsed and filled him with confident strength. "*You* know what I am. You better than anyone else." It was a sly reminder of their curious furtive behavior together; like the hand on her arm, it had its effect. "After all, why do we quarrel the way we did last night?" He hurried on; the job of the rowel was to spur her to action, not to inflame a wound. "Because we're *important* to each other. I know that you would count on me to help if you were in trouble. And I know that you'd be hurt—deeply, Gala!—if I didn't count on you."

She sniffled and scuffed the bright strap over her open-toed sandal.

Then she met his eyes.

It was the after-effect of the quarrel, of course; Glenn Tropile knew just how heavily he could count on the after-spiral of a quarrel. She was submitting.

She glanced furtively at Citizen Boyne and lowered her voice. "What do I have to do?" she whispered.

In five minutes she was gone, but that was more than enough time; Tropile had at least thirty minutes left. They would take Boyne first, he had seen to that. And once Boyne was gone—

Tropile wrenched a leg off his three-legged stool, and sat precariously balanced on the other two. He tossed the loose leg clattering into a corner.

The Keeper of the House of the Five Regulations ambled slack-bodied by and glanced into the room. "Wolf, what happened to your stool?"

Tropile made a left-handed sign: *no importance*. "It doesn't matter. Except it *is* hard to meditate, sitting on this thing, with every muscle tensing and fighting against every other to keep my balance. . . ."

The Keeper made an overruling sign: *please-let-me-help*. "It's your last half hour, Wolf," he reminded Tropile. "I'll fix the stool for you." He entered and slammed and banged it together, and left with an expression of mild concern. Even a Son of the Wolf was entitled to the fullest appreciation of that unique opportunity for meditation, the last half hour before a Donation.

In five minutes he was back, looking solemn and yet glad, like a bearer of serious but welcome tidings. "It is the time for the first Donation," he announced. "Which of you—"

"Him," said Tropile quickly, pointing. Boyne opened his eyes calmly and nodded. He got to his feet, made a formal leavetaking bow to Tropile, and followed the Keeper toward his Donation and his death. As they were going out Tropile coughed a minor supplication. The Keeper paused. "What is it, Wolf?"

Tropile showed him the empty water pitcher—empty, all right; he had emptied it out the window.

"My apologies," the Keeper said, blushing, and hurried Boyne along. He came back almost at once to fill it. He didn't even wait to watch the ceremonial Donation.

Tropile stood watching him, his sub-adrenals beginning to pound like the rolling boil of Well-Aged Water. The Keeper was at a disadvantage. He had been neglectful of his charge—a broken stool; no water in the pitcher. And a Citizen, brought up in a Citizen's mores of consideration and tact, could not help but be humiliated, seek to make amends.

Tropile pressed his advantage home. "Wait," he said winsomely to the Keeper. "I'd like to talk to you."

The Keeper hesitated, torn. "The Donation—"

"Damn the Donation," Tropile said calmly. "After all, what is it but sticking a pipe into a man's backbone and sucking out the juice that keeps him alive? It's killing, that's all."

Crash, crash, crash. The Keeper turned literally white. Tropile was speaking blasphemy, and he wasn't stopping.

"I want to tell you about my wife," Tropile went on, assuming a confidential air. "You know, there's a real woman. Not one of those frozen-up Citizenesses, you know? Why, she and I used to—" He hesitated. "You're a man of the world, aren't you?" he demanded. "I mean, you've seen life."

"I—suppose so," the Keeper said faintly.

"Then you won't be shocked, I know," Tropile lied. "Well, let me tell you, there's a lot to women that these stuffed-shirt Citizens don't know about. Boy! Ever see a woman's knee?" He sniggered. "Ever kiss one, with—" He winked—"*with* the light on? Ever sit in a big arm-chair, say, with a woman in your *lap?* —all soft and heavy, and kind of warm, and slumped up against your chest, you know, and—" He stopped and swallowed; he was almost making himself retch; it was hard to say these things. But he forced himself to go on: "Well, she and I used to do those things. Plenty. All the time. That's what I call a real *woman.*"

He stopped—warned by the Keeper's sudden change of expression, glazed eyes, strangling breath. He had gone too far. He had only wanted to paralyze the man, revolt him, put him out of commission; but he was overdoing it; he jumped forward and caught the Keeper as he fell, fainting.

Callously Tropile emptied the water pitcher over the man.

The Keeper sneezed and sat up groggily.

He focused his eyes on Tropile, and abruptly blushed.

Tropile said harshly: "I wish to see the new sun from the street."

The request was incredible! The Keeper could not possibly allow dangerous liberties to a guest; that was not Citizenship, since the job of a Keeper was to Keep. But Tropile's filthy mouth had unsettled Citizen Harmane.

He floundered, choking on the obscenities he had heard. He was torn between two courses of action, both all but obligatory, both all but impossible. Tropile was in detention regarding the Fifth Regulation. That was all there was to it—looked at from one point of view. Such persons were not to be released from their quarters: the Keeper knew it, the world knew it, Tropile knew it.

It was an obscenity almost greater than the lurid tales of perverted lust, for Tropile had asked something which was impossible! No one *ever* asked anything that was impossible to grant—for no one could ever *refuse* anything; that was utterly graceless, unthinkable.

One could only attempt to compromise. The Keeper stammeringly said: "May I—May I let you see the new sun from the corridor?" And even that was wretchedly wrong; but he had to offer something. One always offered something. The Keeper had never since babyhood given a flat "no" to anybody about anything. No Citizen had. A flat "no" led to hard feelings, strong words—imaginably, even *blows*.

The only flat "no" conceivable was the enormous, terminal "no" of an amok. Short of that—

One offered. One split the difference. One was invariably filled with tepid pleasure when, invariably, the offer was accepted, the difference was split, both parties were satisfied.

"That will do for a start," Tropile snarled. "Open, man, open! Don't make me wait."

The Keeper reeled and unlatched the door to the corridor.

"Now the street!"

"I can't!" burst in an anguished cry from the Keeper. He buried his face in his hands and began to sob, hopelessly incapacitated.

"The street!" Tropile said remorselessly. He felt himself wrenchingly ill; he was going against custom that had ruled his own life as surely as the Keeper's.

But he was Wolf. "I *will* be Wolf," he growled, and advanced upon the Keeper. "My wife," he said, "I didn't finish telling you. Sometimes she used to put her arm around me and just snuggle up and—I remember one time—she kissed my ear. Broad daylight. It felt funny and warm, I can't describe it."

Whimpering, the Keeper flung the keys at Tropile and tottered brokenly away.

He was out of the action. Tropile himself was nearly as badly off; the difference was that he continued to function. The words coming from him seared like acid in his throat. "They call me Wolf," he said aloud, reeling against the wall. "I will be one."

He unlocked the outer door and his wife

was waiting, the things he had asked her to bring in her arms.

Tropile said strangely to her: "I am steel and fire. I am Wolf, full of the old moxie."

She wailed: "Glenn, are you sure I'm doing the right thing?" He laughed unsteadily and led her by the arm through the deserted streets.

5

Citizen Germyn, as was his right by position and status as a connoisseur, helped prepare Citizen Boyne for his Donation. There was nothing much that needed to be done, actually. This made it an elaborate and lengthy task, according to the ethic of the Citizens; it had to be protracted, each step was surrounded by fullest dress of ritual.

It was done in the broad daylight of the new Sun, and as many of the three hundred citizens of Wheeling as could manage it were in the courtyard of the old Federal Building to watch.

The nature of the ceremony was this: A man who revealed himself Wolf, or who finally crumbled under the demands of life and ran amok, could not be allowed to live. He was haled before an audience of his equals and permitted—with the help of force, if that should be necessary, but preferably not—to make the

53

Donation of Spinal Fluid. Execution was murder; and murder was not permitted under the gentle code of Citizens. So this was not execution. The draining of a man's spinal fluid did not kill him. It only insured that, after a time and with much suffering, his internal chemistry would so arrange itself that he would die.

Once the Donation was made the problem was completely altered, of course; suffering was agreed to be a bad thing in itself. So, to save the Donor from the suffering that lay ahead, it was the custom to have the oldest and gentlest Citizen on hand stand by with a sharp-edged knife. When the Donation was complete, the Donor's head was lopped off. It was done purely to avert suffering. Therefore that was not execution either, but only the hastening of an inevitable end. The dozen or so Citizens whose rank permitted them to assist then solemnly dissolved the spinal fluids in water and ceremoniously drank the potion down, at which time it was proper to offer a small poem in commentary. All in all, it was a perfectly splendid opportunity for the second purest form of meditation (other than those on connectivity) by everyone concerned.

Citizen Germyn, whose role was Catheter Bearer, took his place behind the Introducer Bearer, the Annunciators, and the Questioner of Purpose. As he passed Citizen Boyne, Germyn assisted him to assume the proper crouched-over position; Boyne: looked up gratefully and Germyn found the occasion proper for a Commendatory Half-Smile. The Questioner of Purpose said solemnly to Boyne:

"It is your privilege to make a Donation here today. Do you wish to do so?"

"I do," said Boyne raptly. The anxiety had passed; clearly he was confident of making a good Donation; Germyn approved with all his heart.

The Annunciators, in alternate stanzas, announced the proper pause for meditation to the meager crowd, and all fell silent. Citizen Germyn began the process of blanking out his mind, to ready himself for the great opportunity to Appreciate that lay ahead. A sound distracted him; he glanced up irritably. It seemed to come from the House of the Five Regulations, a man's voice, carrying. But no one else appeared to notice it. All of the watchers, all of those on the stone steps, were in somber meditation.

Germyn tried to return his thoughts to where they belonged. . . .

But something was troubling him. He had caught a glimpse of the Donor, and there had been something—something—

He angrily permitted himself to look up once more to see just what it had been about Citizen Boyne that had attracted his attention.

Yes, there was something. Over the form of Citizen Boyne, silent, barely visible, a flicker of life and motion. Nothing tangible. It was as if the air itself were in motion. . . .

It was—Germyn thought with a bursting heart—it was an Eye!

The veritable miracle of Translation, it was about to take place here and now, upon the person of Citizen Boyne! And no one knew it but himself!

In this last surmise Citizen Germyn was wrong.

True, no other human eyes saw the flawed-glass thing that twisted the air over Boyne's prostrate body; but there was, in a sense, another witness some thousands of miles away.

The Pyramid on Mount Everest "stirred."

It did not move; but something about it moved, or changed, or radiated. The Pyramid surveyed its—cabbage patch? Wrist-watch mine? It would make as much sense, it may be, to say wrist-watch patch or cabbage mine; at any rate; it surveyed what to it was a place where intricate mechanisms grew, ripened and were dug up at the moment of usefulness, whereupon they were quick-frozen and wired into circuits.

Through signals perceptible to it, the Pyramid had become "aware" that one of its mechanisms was now ready.

The Pyramid's blood was dielectric fluid. Its limbs were electrostatic charges. Its philosophy was, Unscrew it and push. Its motive was survival.

Survival today was not what survival once had been, for a Pyramid. Once survival had merely been gliding along on a cushion of repellent charges, streaming electrons behind for the push, sending h-f pulses out often enough to get a picture of their bounced return integrated deep inside oneself.

If the picture showed something metabolizable, one metabolized it. One broke it down into molecules by lashing it with the surplus protons left over from the dispersed electrons; one absorbed the molecules. Sometimes the metabolizable object was an Immobile and sometimes a Mobile—a vague, theoretical, frivolous classification to a philosophy whose basis was that *everything* unscrewed. If it was a Mobile one sometimes had to move after it; that was the difference.

The essential was survival, not making idle distinctions.

However, the Pyramids had learned, quite a long time ago, that some distinctions were very useful to make. For example, there was the difference between things that were merely metabolizable and things which, very handily, were assimilable. Quite a lot of effort could be saved if things could simply be "wired" into the places where they were needed, intact.

Well, more or less intact.

This planet was rich in assimilable things. These things had proven well suited to being incorporated right into the functions of the Pyramids' elaborate devices, with hardly any processing at all bar the suppression of unnecessary "needs" or "desires."

It was for this reason that the Pyramids had bothered to steal the planet in the first place.

So the Pyramid on Mount Everest sat and waited.

It was not lonely in its isolation—no Pyramid had ever learned how to be "lonely." For that matter, it was not really alone, either, since its directives came from the binary planet, with which—with all of which, fellow-Pyramids and self-acting devices and all—the Pyramid on Mount Everest was continuously in contact. It sent its h-f pulses bouncing and scattering out. It scattered them additionally on their return. Deep inside, the more-than-anamorphically distorted picture was reintegrated. Deeper inside still, it was interpreted and evaluated for its part in survival, in the sense that the Pyramids had come to understand survival.

"Survival" included the need for the complex components—a human being might have thought of them as "servomechanisms"—which could be assimilated, and which grew wild here.

The planet was, in fact, very rich in these components, and they had a useful habit of "ripening" —which is to say, of becoming perfect for the Pyramids' use—on their own. This occurred, however, at irregular and unpredictable intervals. Therefore the Pyramid on Mount Everest was obliged to maintain a constant surveillance, planet wide, for the perfect moment of plucking.

(Of course, the components being harvested did not know they were ripening to be plucked. A wrist-watch on a jeweler's shelf doesn't know it is waiting for a shopper to buy it. The shopper has no interest in the previous state of the wrist-watch, either. So it was with the Pyramids and the useful devices they harvested on Earth.)

So when its surveillance showed a component was ripe, the Pyramid plucked it. It used electrostatic charges. When the charges formed about a component about to be plucked, they distorted the refractive index of the air. Human beings called this an "Eye."

The Pyramid now found that a component was ripe for plucking.

A world away from Mount Everest, in Wheeling, West Virginia, Citizen Boyne had attained the rapture of total emptying of the mind. The electrostatic charges over his head swirled into an Eye.

There was a sound like the clapping of two hands, or a small thunder-crash.

The Citizens of Wheeling knew that sound well. It was the miniature thunderclap of air slapping together, as it filled the space that had been occupied by the kneeling, meditating form of Citizen Boyne, raptly awaiting his Donation of Fluid.

The three hundred Citizens of Wheeling were jerked out of their own meditations by the sound. They gasped in envy and admiration (and perhaps, a little, in fear) as they saw that Citizen Boyne had been Translated.

Or, put in a different context, that Citizen Boyne had become ripe and therefore was harvested.

6

Glenn Tropile and his sobbing wife lay down for the night in the stubble of a cornfield. Gala Tropile ultimately fell asleep, still whimpering softly in her dreams. Her husband found sleep harder.

Numbed by contact with the iron chill of the field—it would be weeks before the new Sun warmed the earth enough for it to begin radiating in turn—Tropile tossed restlessly. He closed his eyes and tried meditation; it would not work; unwanted visions flashed across his mind. He opened them and tried to meditate that way. Sometimes the heavenly blankness came best when you simply chose to ignore the visual world. . . .

Not this time; when Tropile opened his eyes he saw a bright star just over the horizon. It had not been in the sky lately, but Tropile recognized it at once.

It was the binary planet. It was the home of the Pyramids.

Tropile shivered with more than cold. No one liked to see that planet in the sky. To look at it was to remind oneself of all the evils that it had brought. To speak of it was unpardonable. Even before the littlest children had learned that one didn't ask for more food or point to another child's genitals, they learned that one *never* mentioned the binary planet, however bright it might appear in the sky.

Its evil was lessened, microscopically, by the fact that it had no light of its own. Like any planet; like Mars or Jupiter or all the lost others, it shone only by reflection of the light from the nearest self-luminous body, in this case, Earth's sunlet. So it was brightest when one could stand its hideous presence best—at the time of the Re-Creation of the Sun. And when the old and dying Sun was faint, and everyone was fearful and strained, it could hardly be picked out at all.

That was only a very small mercy, but the basic fact of human life was that there weren't any large ones any more.

Tropile shut his eyes on the unwelcome sight and tried again to sleep. Even when it came it was fitful. He dreamed. He did not enjoy his dreams, because in them he was Wolf.

Half-waking, he knew it was true. Well, let it be so, he told himself again and again; I *will* be Wolf; I will strike back at the Citizens, I will—

Always the thought trailed off. He would exactly *what?* What could he do?

Migration was an answer—go to another city. With Gala, he supposed. Start a new life, where he was not known as Wolf.

And then what? Try to live a sheep's life, as he had tried all his years? And there was the question of whether, in fact, he could manage to find a city where he was not known. The human race was migratory, in these years of subjection to the never-quite-understood rule of the Pyramids. It was a matter of insolation. When the new Sun was young, it was hot, and there was plenty of warmth; it was possible to spread north and south, away from the final line of permafrost which, in North America, came just above the old Mason-Dixon line. When the Sun was dying, the cold spread down. The race followed the seasons. Soon all of Wheeling would be spreading north again, and how was he to be sure that none of Wheeling's citizens might not turn up wherever he might go?

He was not to be sure, that was the answer to that.

All right, scratch migration. What remained?

He could—with Gala, he guessed—live a solitary life, on the fringes of cultivated land. They both had some skill at rummaging the old storehouses of the ancients.

It took skill. Plundering the old supermarkets was not only bad manners—terminally bad—it was also dangerous. You could die of poisoning if you didn't know what you were doing. Over the centuries, nearly all of the most interesting canned goods had decayed themselves into lethal and repellent mixtures. However, that did not mean there was nothing there. For reasons known only to themselves, the ancients had seen fit to take some kinds of foodstuffs which kept well enough by themselves, and go on to seal them into vacuum-tight cans. Crackers. Pasta. Unleavened bread—yes, there were lots of things still there.

So it was possible.

But even a Wolf is gregarious by nature; and there were bleak hours in that night when Tropile found himself close to sobbing with his wife.

At the first break of dawn he was up. Gala had fallen into a light and restless sleep; he called her awake. "We have to move," he said harshly. "Maybe they'll get enough guts to follow us. I don't want them to find us."

Silently she got up. They rolled and tied the blankets she had brought; they ate quickly from the food she had brought; they made packs and put them on their shoulders, and started to walk. One thing in their favor: They were moving fast, faster than any Citizen was likely to follow. All the same, Tropile kept looking nervously behind him.

They hurried north and east, and that was a mistake; because by noon they found themselves blocked by water. It was impassable. They would have to skirt it westward until they found a bridge or a boat.

"We can stop and eat," Tropile said grudgingly, trying not to despair.

They slumped to the ground. It was warmer now; Tropile found himself getting drowsier, drowsier— He jerked erect and stared around belligerently. Beside him his wife was lying motionless, though her eyes were open, gazing at the sky. Tropile sighed and stretched out. A moment's rest, he promised himself. And then a quick bite to eat, and then onward. . . . He was sound asleep when they came for him.

There was a flutter of iron bird's wings from overhead.

Tropile jumped up out of sleep, awakening to panic. It was outside the possibility of belief, but there it was: In the sky over him, etched black against a cloud, a helicopter. And men staring out of it, staring down at him.

A helicopter!

But there were no helicopters, or none that flew—if there had been fuel to fly them with—if any man had had the skill to make them fly. It was impossible! And yet there it was, and the men were looking at him, and the impossible great whirling thing was coming down, nearer.

He began to run in the downward wash of air from the vanes. But it was no use. There were three men, and they were fresh, and he wasn't. He stopped, dropping into the fighter's crouch that is pre-set into the human body, ready to do battle. They didn't want to fight. They laughed. One of them said amiably, "*Long* past your bedtime, boy. Get in. We'll take you home."

Tropile stood poised, hands half-clenched and half-clawed. "Take—"

"Take you home. Yeah." The man nodded. "Where you belong, Tropile, you know? Not back to Wheeling, if that's what is worrying you."

"Where I—"

"Where you belong." Then he understood.

He got into the helicopter wonderingly. Home. Then there *was* a home for such as he. He wasn't alone, he needn't keep his solitary self apart; he could be with his own kind. "How," he began, rummaging through the long list of questions he needed to put, and settling for, "How did you know my name?"

The man laughed. "Did you think you were the only Wolf in Wheeling? We keep our eyes open, Tropile. We have to; that's what Wolves are like." And then, as Tropile opened his mouth for another question, "If you're wondering about your wife, I think she must have heard us coming before you did. I think we saw her about half a mile from here, back along your track. Heading back to Wheeling as fast as she could go."

Tropile nodded. That was better, after all; Gala was no Wolf, though he had tried his best to make her one.

One of the men closed the door; another did something with levers and wheels; the vanes whooshed around overhead; the helicopter bounced on its stiff-sprung landing legs and then rocked up and away.

For the first time in his life Glenn Tropile looked *down* on the land.

They didn't fly high—but Glenn Tropile had never flown at all, and the two or three hundred feet of air beneath him made him faint and queasy. They danced through the passes in the West Virginia hills, crossed icy streams and rivers, swung past old empty towns which no longer had even names of their own. They saw no one.

It was something over four hundred miles to where they were going, so one of the men told him. They made it easily before dark.

Tropile walked through the town in the evening light. Electricity flared white and violet in the buildings around him. Imagine! Electricity was calories, and calories were to be hoarded.

There were other walkers in the street. Their gait was not the economical shuffle with pendant arms. They burned energy visibly. They swung. They *strode*. It had been painted on his brain in earliest childhood that such walking was wrong, reprehensible, silly, debilitating. It wasted calories. These people did not look debilitated, and they didn't seem to mind wasting calories.

It was an ordinary sort of town, apparently named Princeton. It did not have the transient look to it of, say, Wheeling, or Altoona, or Gary, in Tropile's experience. It looked like—

well, it looked permanent. Tropile had heard of a town called Princeton but it happened that he had never passed through it southwarding or northbound. There was no reason why he or anybody should have or should not have. Still, there was a possibility, once he thought of it, that things were somehow so arranged that they should not; perhaps it was all on purpose. Like every town it was underpopulated, but not as much so as most. Perhaps one living space in five was used. A high ratio.

The man beside him was named Haendl, one of the men from the helicopter. They hadn't talked much on the flight and they didn't talk much now. "Eat first," Haendl said, and took Tropile to a bright and busy sort of food stall. Only it wasn't a stall, it was a restaurant.

This Haendl, what to make of him? He should have been disgusting, nasty, an abomination. He had no manners whatever. He didn't know, or at least didn't use, the Seventeen Conventional Gestures. He wouldn't let Tropile walk behind him and to his left, though he was easily five years Tropile's senior. When he ate, he *ate*; the Sip of Appreciation, the Pause of First Surfeit, the Thrice Proffered Share meant nothing to him; he laughed when Tropile tried to give him the Elder's Portion.

Cheerfully patronizing, this man Haendl said to Tropile: "That stuff's all right when you don't have anything better to do with your time. You poor mutts don't. You'd die of boredom without your inky-pinky cults, and you don't have the resources to do anything bigger. Yes, I do know the Gestures. Seventeen delicate ways of communicating emotions too refined for words to express—or too dangerous! The hell with all of that, Tropile. I've got words, and I'm not afraid to use them. Saves time. You'll learn; we all did."

"But," said Tropile, trying frantically to rebalance the budget of behavior in his mind, "what about *waste*? What about the need to economize on food? Where does it all come from?"

"We steal it from the sheep," the man said brutally. "You'll do it too. Now why don't you just shut up and eat?"

Tropile ate silently, trying to think.

A man arrived, *threw* himself in a chair, glanced curiously at Tropile and said: "Haendl, the Somerville Road. The creek backed up when it froze. Flooded, bad. Ruined everything."

Tropile ventured: "The flood ruined the road?"

"The road? No. Say, you must be the fellow Haendl went after? Tropile, that's the name?" He leaned across the table, pumped Tropile's hand. "We had the road nicely blocked," he explained. "The flood washed it clean. Now we have to block it again."

Haendl said: "Take the tractor if you need it." The man nodded and left. Haendl said, "Eat up, we're wasting time. About that road.

We keep them blocked up, see? Why let a lot of Sheep in and out?"

"Sheep?"

"The opposite," said Haendl, "of Wolves."

Haendl explained. Take ten billion people, and say that out of every million of them, one—just one—is different. He has a talent for survival; call him Wolf. Ten thousand of him, in a world of ten billion.

Squeeze them, freeze them, cut them down. Let old *Rejoice-in-Messias* loom in the terrifying sky and so abduct the earth that the human race is decimated, fractionated, reduced to what is in comparison a bare handful of chilled, stunned survivors. There aren't ten billion people in the world any more. No, not by a factor of a thousand. Maybe there are as many as ten million, more or less, rattling around in the space their enormous Elder Generations made for them.

And of these ten million, how many are Wolf?

Ten thousand.

"You understand, Tropile. *We survive*. I don't care what you call us. The Sheep call us Wolves, and me, I kind of like to call us Supermen. But we survive."

Tropile nodded, beginning to understand. "The way I survived the House of the Five Regulations."

Haendl gave him a pitying look. "The way you survived thirty years of Sheephood before that. Come on."

It was a tour of inspection. They went into a

building, big, looking like any other big and useless building of the ancients, gray stone walls, windows with ragged shards of glass. Only inside it wasn't like the others. Two sub-basements down, Tropile winced and turned away from the flood of violet light that poured out of a quartz bulls-eye on top of a squat steel cone. "Perfectly harmless, Tropile, you don't have to worry," Haendl boomed. "Know what you're looking at? There's a fusion reactor down there. Heat. Power. All the power we need. Do you know what that means?" He stared somberly down at the flaring violet light of the inspection port. "Come on," he said abruptly.

Another building, also big, also gray stone. A cracked inscription over the entrance read: "—ORIAL HALL OF HUMANITIES." The sense-shock this time was not light, it was sound. Hammering, screeching, rattling, rumbling. Men were doing noisy things with metal and machines. "Repair shop!" Haendl yelled. "See those machines? They belong to our man Innison. We've salvaged them from every big factory ruin we could find. Give Innison a piece of metal—any alloy, any shape—and one of those machines will change it into any other shape and damned near any other alloy. Drill it, cut it, plane it, weld it, smelt it, zone-melt it, bond it—you tell him what to do and he'll do it. We got the parts to make six tractors and forty-one cars out of this shop. And we've got other shops—aircraft in Farmingdale and Wichita, armaments in Wilmington. Not that we can't make some armaments here. Innison

could build you a tank if he had to, complete
with one-oh-five millimeter gun."

Tropile said: "What's a tank?"

Haendl only looked at him and said: "Come
on!"

Tropile's head spun dizzily and all the spec-
tacles merged and danced in his mind. They
were incredible. All of them.

Fusion pile, machine shop, vehicular ga-
rage, aircraft hangar. There was a storeroom
under the seats of a football stadium, and
Tropile's head spun on his shoulders again as
he tried to count the cases of coffee and canned
soups and whisky and beans. There was another storeroom, only this one was called an
armory. It was filled with . . . guns. Guns that
could be loaded with cartridges, of which they
had very many; guns which, when you loaded
them and pulled the trigger, would fire.

Tropile said, remembering: "I saw a gun
once that still had its firing pin. But it was
rusted solid."

"These work, Tropile. You can kill a man
with them. Some of us have."

"*Kill*—"

"Get that Sheep look out of your eyes,
Tropile! What's the difference how you exe-
cute a criminal? And what's a criminal but
someone who represents a danger to your
world? We prefer a gun instead of the Donation of the Spinal Tap, because it's quicker,
because it's less messy—and because we don't
like to drink spinal fluid, no matter what imag-

inary therapeutic or symbolic value it has. You'll learn."

But he didn't add "come on." They had arrived where they were going.

It was a small room in the building that housed the armory, and it held, among other things, a rack of guns.

"Sit down," said Haendl, taking one of the guns out of the rack thoughtfully and caressing it as the doomed Boyne had his watch-case. It was the latest pre-Pyramid model rifle, anti-personnel, short-range. It would not bunch a cluster of shots in a coffee can at much more than two and a half miles.

"All right," said Haendl, stroking the stock. "You've seen the works, Tropile. You've lived thirty years with Sheep; you've seen what they have and what we have; I don't have to ask you to make a choice. I know what you choose. The only thing left is to tell you what *we* want from *you*."

A faint pulsing began inside of Glenn Tropile. "I expected we'd be getting to that."

"Why not? We're not Sheep. We don't act that way. *Quid pro quo*. Remember that, it saves time. You've seen the *quid*. Now we come to the *quo*." He leaned forward. "Tropile, what do you know about the Pyramids?"

"Nothing," Tropile said promptly.

Haendl nodded. "Right. They're all around us and our lives are beggared because of them. And we don't even know why. We don't know what they are. Did you know that one of the

Sheep was Translated in Wheeling when you left?"

"Translated?" Tropile listened with his mouth open while Haendl told him about what had happened to Citizen Boyne. "So he didn't make the Donation after all," he said.

"Might have been better if he had," said Haendl. "We don't know. Still, it gave you a chance to get away. We had heard—never mind how just yet—that Wheeling'd caught itself a Wolf, so we came after you. But you were already gone."

Tropile said, faintly annoyed: "You were damn near too late."

"Oh, no, Tropile. We're never too late. If you don't have enough gumption to get away from Sheep, you're no Wolf; simple as that. But there's this Translation; we know it happens; but we don't even know what *it* is. All we know, people disappear. There's a new sun in the sky every five years or so. Who makes it? The Pyramids. How? We don't know that. Sometimes something floats around in the air, and we call it an Eye. It has something to do with Translation, something to do with the Pyramids. What? We don't know that."

"We don't know much of anything," interrupted Tropile, trying to hurry him along.

"Not about the Pyramids, no." Haendl shook his head. "Hardly anyone has ever seen one, for that matter."

"Hardly— You mean, you have?"

"Oh, yes. There's a Pyramid on Mount Everest, you know. That's not just a story, it's true. I've been there, and it's there. At least, it was there five years ago, right after the last Sun Re-creation. I guess it hasn't moved. It just sits there."

Tropile listened, marveling. To have seen a real Pyramid! Almost he had thought of them as legends, contrived to account for such established physical facts as the Eyes and Translations, as children account for gifts at Ecksmass with Kringle-San. But this incredible man had seen it!

"Somebody dropped a H-bomb on it, way back," Haendl went on, "and the only thing that happened is that now the North Col is a crater. You can't move it. You can't hurt it. But it's alive. It has been there, alive, for a couple of hundred years; and that's about all we know about the Pyramids. Right?"

"Right."

Haendl stood up. "Tropile, that's what all of this is all about!" He gestured around him. "Guns, tanks, airplanes—we want to know more! We're going to find out more, and then we're going to fight."

There was a jarring note, and Tropile caught at it, sniffing the air. Somehow—perhaps it was his sub-adrenals that told him—this very positive, very self-willed man was just the slightest bit unsure of himself. But Haendl swept on and Tropile for a moment forgot to be alert.

"We had a party up Mount Everest five years ago," he was saying. "We didn't find out a thing. Five years before that, and five years before *that*—every time there's a new sun, while it is still warm enough to give a party a chance to climb up the sides, we send a team up there. It's a rough job. We give it to the new boys, Tropile. Like you."

There it was. He was being invited to attack a Pyramid.

Tropile hesitated, delicately balanced, trying to get the *feel* of this negotiation. This was Wolf against Wolf; it was hard. There had to be an advantage—

"There is an advantage," Haendl said aloud.

Tropile jumped, but then he remembered: Wolf against Wolf. Haendl went on: "What you get out of it is your life, in the first place. You understand you can't get out now. We don't want Sheep meddling around. And in the second place, there's a considerable hope of gain." He stared at Tropile with a dreamer's eyes. "We don't send parties up there for nothing, you know. We want to get something out of it. What we want is the earth."

"The earth?" It reeked of madness; but this man wasn't mad.

"Some day, Tropile, it's going to be us against them. Never mind the Sheep, they don't count. It's going to be Pyramids and Wolves, and the Pyramids won't win. And then—"

It was enough to curdle the blood. This man was proposing to *fight*, and against the invulnerable, the almost godlike Pyramids, at that!

But he was glowing, and the fever was contagious. Tropile felt his own blood begin to pound. Haendl hadn't finished his "and then—", but he didn't have to. The "and then" was obvious: And then the world takes up again from the day the wandering planet first came into view. And then we, somehow, learn how to drive this old planet right back to its own solar system. And then we put an end to the five-year cycle of frost and hunger. And then—

And then the world would be worth living in again, and it would be Wolves who would rule it.

"By God, Haendl," cried Glenn Tropile, "I believe it can happen!"

Haendl merely smiled and nodded.

"I'll do it!" Tropile amplified. He raced on, "Let's see, every new expedition to Mount Everest tries some new weapon against the Pyramid, right? Okay. What's left? We know nukes won't work. I suppose if that's true then no chemical explosion could do any damage to it. What about acids? Subsonic vibrations? What about, I don't know, some kind of germ warfare? I can see that I'll want to talk to the people who have been on the previous expeditions right away—"

He stopped in midflight. The smile on Haendl's face had taken on a disturbingly lacquered appearance, as though the man were trying to preserve it. The voice was overhearty, too: "I'll get you all the transcripts of their radio reports, Tropile."

Tropile studied him carefully for a moment. When he spoke his voice was quite calm. "Which means, I guess," he said, "that none of those people got back alive to talk to, right?

But you said you'd actually seen the Pyramid yourself."

"Well, I did!" said Haendl, and then added lamely, "Through a telescope, from the five-thousand-foot base camp."

"I see," said Tropile mildly.

Then he laughed.

What difference did it make, anyway? If this whole enterprise was really all very silly, it was also, at least, a new kind of thing to think about. Its promises might be false. But they also might not be—or it might be possible to find something real amid all the dreamy hopes and self-deceptions. Glenn Tropile was Wolf. He would do his best to find a way of getting an advantage in any circumstances. If one thing failed he would try another, and this was something new to try.

Besides, it was the only game in town.

Tropile grinned at Haendl. "You can put away the gun, friend. You've signed me up."

7

The year began again, a year that ran for one thousand, eight hundred and twenty-five days on the calendar, for forty-three thousand and eight hundred hours on the clock. First came some thirty days of spring, during which the renewed sunlet poured heat into the ice and oceans and rocks, which greedily absorbed it. Ice melted, oceans warmed, and rocks at last were no longer frozen to the touch but gently warm.

Ten million citizens stirred to spring; once more they had survived. Farmers scratched the ground again, charcoal burners ritually sealed their kilns and put their hands to carpentry or roadmending for a while, and fifteen hundred devotees of the Ice Cult started their pilgrimages from all over North America to see the breakup at Niagara.

Then after thirty days it was summer, long and sweltering. Plants burst forth for reaping

and the farmers swiftly stirred their soil and
planted again, and reaped again, and planted
for the last time. The coastal cities as usual
were inundated by the spreading floods from
the polar caps, furnishing refined pleasure to
those who fancied Submergence. A fine year,
they told one another; a vintage year—the flat
top of the Lever Building vanishing from sight
under a sunset blaze!

And through the spring and summer Glenn
Tropile learned how to be a Wolf.

The way, he glumly found, lay through su-
pervising the colony's nursery school. It wasn't
what he had expected, but it had the advantage that while his charges were learning, he
was learning too.

One jump ahead of the three-year-olds, he
found that the "wolves," far from being preda-
tors on the "sheep," existed with them in a far
more complicated ecological relationship. There
were Wolves all through sheepdom; they leav-
ened the dough of society.

In barbarously simple prose a primer said:
"The Sons of the Wolf are good at numbers
and money. You and your friends play money
games almost as soon as you can talk, and you
can think in percentages and compound interest when you want to. Most people are not
able to do this."

True, thought Tropile sub-vocally, reading
aloud to the tots. That was how it had been
with him.

"Sheep are afraid of the Sons of the Wolf.
Those of us who live among them are in con-

stant danger of detection and death—although ordinarily a Wolf can take care of himself against any number of Sheep." True, too.

"It is one of the most dangerous assignments a Wolf can be given to live among the Sheep. Yet it is essential. Without us, they would die—of stagnation, of rot, eventually of hunger."

It didn't have to be spelled out any further. Sheep can't mend their own fences.

The prose was horrifyingly bald and the children were horrifyingly—he choked on the word, but managed to form it in his mind—*competitive*. The verbal taboos lingered, he found, after he had broken through the barriers of behavior.

But it was distressing, in a way. At an age when future Citizens would have been learning their Little Pitcher Ways, these children were learning to fight. The perennial argument about who would get to be Big Bill Zeckendorf when they played a strange game called "Zeckendorf and Hilton" sometimes ended in bloody noses.

And nobody—nobody at all—meditated on connectivity.

Tropile was warned not to do it himself. Haendl said grimly: "We don't understand it, and we don't like what we don't understand. We're suspicious animals, Tropile. As the children grow older we give them just enough practice so they can go into one meditation and get the feel of it—or pretend to, at any rate. If they have to pass as Citizens they'll need that much. But more than that we do not allow."

"Allow?" Somehow the word grated; somehow his sub-adrenals began to pulse.

"Allow! We have our suspicions, and we know for a fact that sometimes people disappear when they meditate. There's that much truth in the sheep talk about Translation. We don't want to disappear. We judge that it is not a good thing to disappear. Don't meditate, Tropile. You hear?"

But later, he had to argue the point. He picked a time when Haendl was free, or as nearly free as that man ever was. The whole adult colony had been out on what they used as a parade ground—once it had been a "football field," Haendl said. They had done their regular twice-a-week infantry drill, that being one of the prices one paid for living among the free, progressive Wolves instead of the dull and tepid Sheep. Tropile was mightily winded, but he cast himself on the ground near Haendl, caught his breath and said: "Haendl, about Meditation."

"What about it?"

"Well, perhaps you don't really grasp it." He searched for words. He knew what he wanted to say. How could anything that felt as good as Oneness be bad? And wasn't Translation, after all, so rare as hardly to matter? But he wasn't sure he could get through to Haendl in those terms. He tried: "When you meditate successfully, Haendl, you're one with the universe. Do you know what I mean? There's no feeling like it. It's indescribable peace, beauty, harmony, repose."

"It's the world's cheapest narcotic," Haendl snorted.

"Oh, now, really—"

"*And* the world's cheapest religion. The stone-broke mutts can't afford gilded idols, so they use their own navels. That's all it is. They can't afford alcohol; they can't even afford the muscular exertion of deep breathing that would throw them into a state of hyperventilated oxygen drunkenness. So what's left? Self-hypnosis. Nothing else. It's all they can do, so they learn it, they define it as pleasant and good, and they're all fixed up."

Tropile sighed. The man was *so* stubborn. Then a thought occurred to him, and he pushed himself up on his elbows. "Aren't you leaving something out? What about Translation?"

Haendl glowered at him. "That's the part we don't understand."

"But surely, self-hypnosis doesn't account for—"

"Surely, it doesn't!" Haendl mimicked savagely. "All right. We don't understand it, and we're afraid of it. Kindly do not tell me Translation is the supreme act of Un-willing, Total Disavowal of Duality, Unison with the Brahm-Ground or any such schlock. You don't know what it is; and neither do we." He started to get up. "All we know is, people vanish. And we want no part of it; so we don't meditate. None of us—including you!"

*   *   *

It was foolishness, this close-order drill. Could you defeat the unreachable Himalayan Pyramid with a squads-right flanking maneuver?

And yet it wasn't all foolishness. Close-order drill and 3500-calorie-a-day diet began to put fat and flesh and muscle on Tropile's body, and something other than that on his mind. He had not lost the edge of his acquisitiveness, his drive—his whatever-it-was that made the difference between Wolf and Sheep. But he had gained something. Happiness? Well, if "happiness" is a sense of purpose, and a hope that the purpose can be accomplished, then happiness. It was a feeling that had never existed in his life before. Always it had been the glandular compulsion to gain an advantage, and that was gone, or anyway almost gone; because it was permitted in the society in which he now lived.

Glenn Tropile sang as he putt-putted in his tractor, plowing the thawing Jersey fields. Still, a faint doubt remained. Squads-right against the Pyramids?

Stiffly, Tropile stopped the tractor, slowed the Diesel to a steady *thrum* and got off. It was hot—being mid-summer of the five-year calendar the Pyramids had imposed. It was time for rest and maybe something to eat.

He sat in the shade of a tree, as farmers always have, and opened his sandwiches. He was only a mile or so from Princeton, but he might as well have been in Limbo; there was no sign of any living human but himself. The

northering Sheep didn't come near Princeton—
it "happened" that way, on purpose. He caught
a glimpse of something moving, but when he
stood up for a better look into the woods on
the other side of the field, it was gone. Wolf?
Real wolf, that is? It could have been a bear,
for that matter—there was talk of wolves and
bears around Princeton; and although Tropile
knew that much of the talk was assiduously
encouraged by men like Haendl, he also knew
that some of it was true.

As long as he was up, he gathered straw
from the litter of last "year's" head-high grass,
gathered sticks under the trees, built a small
fire, and put water on to boil for coffee. Then
he sat back and ate his sandwiches, thinking.

Maybe it was a promotion, going from the
nursery school to labor in the fields. Haendl
had promised a place in the expedition that
would, maybe, discover something new and
great and helpful about the Pyramids. And
that might still come to pass, because the expedition was far from ready to leave.

Tropile munched his sandwiches thoughtfully. Now, *why* was the expedition so far from
ready to leave? It was absolutely essential to
get there in the warmest weather possible—
otherwise Everest was unclimbable; generations of alpinists had proved that. That warmest
weather was rapidly going by.

Uneasily he put a few more sticks on the
fire, staring thoughtfully into the canteen-cup
of water. It was a satisfyingly hot fire, he

noticed abstractedly. The water was very nearly ready to boil.

Half across the world, the Pyramid in the Himalayas felt, or heard, or tasted—a difference.

Possibly the h-f pulses that had gone endlessly wheep, wheep, wheep were now going wheep-*beep*, wheep-*beep*. Possibly the electromagnetic "taste" of lower-than-red was now spiced with a tang of beyond-violet. Whatever the sign was, the Pyramid recognized it.

A part of the crop it tended was ready to harvest.

The ripening bud had a name, but names didn't matter to the Pyramid. The man named Tropile didn't know he was ripening, either. All that Tropile knew was that for the first time in nearly a year, he had succeeded in catching each stage of the nine perfect states of water-coming-to-a-boil in its purest form.

It was like . . . like . . . well, it was like nothing that anyone but a Water-Watcher could understand. He observed. He appreciated. He encompassed and absorbed the myriad subtle perfections of time, of shifting transparency, of sound, of distribution of ebulliency, of the faint, faint odor of steam.

Complete, Glenn Tropile relaxed all his limbs and let his chin rest on his breast-bone.

It was, he thought with placid, crystalline perception, a rare and perfect opportunity for meditation. He thought of connectivity. (Overhead a shifting glassy flaw appeared in the thin, still air.) There wasn't any thought of Eyes in the erased palimpsest that was Glenn Tropile's mind. There wasn't any thought of Pyramids or of Wolves. The plowed field before him didn't exist. Even the water, merrily bubbling itself dry, was gone from his perception; he was beginning to meditate.

Time passed—or stood still; for Tropile there was no difference. There was no time. He found himself almost on the brink of Understanding. (The Eye above swirled wildly.)

Something snapped. An intruding blue-bottle drone, or a twitching muscle. Partly Tropile came back to reality, almost he glanced upward, almost he saw the Eye . . .

It didn't matter. The thing that really mattered, the only thing in the world, was all within his mind; and he was ready, he knew, to find it. Once more!

He let the mind-clearing unanswerable question drift into his mind:

If the sound of two hands together is a clapping, what is the sound of one hand?

Gently he pawed at the question, the symbol of the futility of mind—and therefore the gateway to meditation. Unawareness of self was stealing deliciously over him.

He was Glenn Tropile. He was more than that. He was the water boiling . . . and the boiling water was he; he was the gentle warmth of the fire, which was—which was, yes, itself the arc of the sky. As each thing was each other thing; water was fire, and fire air; Tropile was the first simmering bubble and the full roll of well-aged water was Self, was—

The answer to the unanswerable question was coming clearer and softer to him. And then, all at once but not suddenly, for there was no time, it was not close, it *was*. The answer was his, was him, the arc of sky was the answer, and the answer belonged to sky—to warmth, to all warmths that there are, and to all waters, and— and the answer was— was—

Tropile vanished. The mild thunderclap that followed made the flames dance and the column of steam fray; and then the fire was steady again, and so was the rising steam. But Tropile was gone.

8

Haendl plodded angrily through the high grass toward the dull throb of the Diesel.

Maybe it had been a mistake to take this Glenn Tropile into the colony. He was more Citizen than Wolf—no, cancel that, Haendl thought; he was more Wolf than Citizen. But the Wolf in him was tainted with sheep's blood. He *competed* like a Wolf; but in spite of everything he refused to give up some of his sheep's ways. Meditation. He had been cautioned against meditation. But had he given it up?

He had not.

If it had been entirely up to Haendl, Glenn Tropile would have found himself out on his ear, back among the Sheep, or else dead. Fortunately for Tropile, it was not entirely up to Haendl. The community of Wolves was by no means a democracy, but the leader had a certain responsibility to his constituents, and the responsibility was this: He couldn't afford to be wrong. Like the Old Gray Wolf who protected Mowgli, he had to defend his actions against attack; if he failed to defend, the pack would pull him down.

And Innison thought they needed Tropile— not in spite of the taint of the Citizen that he bore, but because of it.

Haendl bawled: "Tropile! Tropile, where are you?" There was only the wind and the *thrum* of the Diesel. It was enormously irritating. Haendl had other things to do than to chase after Glenn Tropile. And where was he? There was the Diesel, idling wastefully; there the end of the patterned furrows Tropile had plowed. There a small fire, burning—

And there was Tropile.

Haendl stopped, frozen, his mouth opened to yell Tropile's name.

It was Tropile, all right, staring with concentrated, oyster-eyed gaze at the fire and the little pot of water it boiled. Staring. Meditating. And over his head, like flawed glass in a pane, was the thing Haendl feared most of all things on Earth. It was an Eye.

Tropile was on the very verge of being Translated . . . whatever that was.

Maybe at last this was the time to find out *what* that was! Haendl ducked back into the shelter of the high grass, knelt, plucked his radio communicator from his pocket, urgently called. "Innison! Innison, will somebody for God's sake put Innison on!" Seconds passed, voices answered; then there was Innison.

"Innison, listen! You wanted to catch Tropile in the act of meditation? All right, you've got him. The old wheat field, south end, under the elms around the creek. Got it? Get here fast, Innison—there's an Eye forming above him!"

Luck! Lucky that they were ready for this, and only by luck, because it was the helicopter that Innison had patiently assembled for the attack on Everest that was ready now, loaded with instruments, planned to weigh and measure the aura around the Pyramid— now at hand when they needed it. That was luck, but there was driving hurry involved too; it was only a matter of minutes before Tropile heard the wobbling drone of the copter, saw the vanes fluttering low over the hedges, dropping to earth behind the elms. Haendl raised himself cautiously and peered. Yes, Tropile was still there, and the Eye still above him! But the noise of the helicopter had frayed the spell; Tropile stirred; the Eye wavered and shook—

But did not vanish.

Thanking what passed for his God, Haendl scuttled circuitously around the elms and joined Innison, furiously closing switches and pointing lenses, at the copter. . . .

They saw Tropile sitting there, the Eye growing larger and closer over his head. They had time—plenty of time; oh, nearly a minute of time. They brought to bear on the silent and unknowing form of Glenn Tropile every instrument that the copter carried. They were waiting for Tropile to disappear—

He did.

Innison and Haendl ducked at the thunderclap as air rushed in to replace him.

"We've got what you wanted," Haendl said harshly. "Let's read some instruments."

Throughout the Translation high-tensile magnetic tape on a madly spinning drum had been hurtling under twenty-four recording heads at a hundred feet a second. Output to the recording heads had been from every kind of measuring device they had been able to conceive and build, all loaded on the helicopter for use on Mount Everest—all now pointed directly at Glenn Tropile. They had, for the instant of Translation, readings from one microsecond to the next on the varying electric, gravitational, magnetic, radiant and molecular-state conditions in his vicinity.

They got back to Innison's workshop and the laboratory inside it in less than a minute; but it took hours of playing back the magnetic pulses into machines that turned them into scribed curves on coördinate paper before Innison had anything resembling an answer.

He said: "No mystery. I mean, no mystery except the speed. Want to know what happened to Tropile?"

"I do," said Haendl.

"A pencil of electrostatic force maintained by a pinch effect bounced down from the approximate azimuth of Everest—God knows how they handled the elevation—and charged him and the area positive. A *big* charge; clear off the scale. They parted company. He was bounced straight up; a meter off the ground, a correcting vector was applied; when last seen he was headed fast in the direction of the Pyramids' binary. Fast, I say. So fast that I would guess he'll get there alive. It takes an appreciable time, a good part of a second, for his protein to coagulate enough to make him sick and then kill him. If they strip the charges off him immediately on arrival, as I should imagine they will, he'll live."

"Friction—"

"Be damned to friction," Innison said calmly. "He carried a packet of air with him and there *was* no friction. How? I don't know. How are they going to keep him alive in space, without the charges that hold the air? I don't know. If they don't maintain the charges, can they beat light speed? I don't know. I tell you what happened, I can't tell you *how*."

Haendl stood up thoughtfully. "It's something," he said grudgingly.

"It's more than we've ever had—a complete reading at the instant of Translation!"

"We'll get more," Haendl promised. "Innison, now you know what to look for. Keep looking for it. Keep every possible detection device monitored twenty-four hours a day. Turn on everything you've got that'll find a sign of imposed modulation. At any sign—or at anybody's hunch that there *might* be a sign—I'm to be called. If I'm eating. If I'm sleeping. If

I'm enjoying the pangs of love. Call me, you hear? Maybe you were right about Tropile; maybe he did have some use. Maybe he'll give the Pyramids a bellyache."

Innison, flipping the magnetic-tape drum to rewind, said thoughtfully: "It's too bad they've got him. We could have used some more readings."

"Too bad?" Haendl laughed sharply. "Maybe not, Innison. This time they've got themselves a Wolf."

The Pyramids did have a Wolf—a datum which did not matter in the least to them.

It is not possible to know what "mattered" to a Pyramid except by inference. But it is possible to know that they had no way of telling Wolf from Citizen.

The planet which was their home—Earth's binary—was small, dark, atmosphereless and waterless. It was honeycombed and packed with a myriad of devices.

In the old days, when technology had followed war, luxury, government and leisure, their sun had run out of steam; and at about the same time the Pyramids had run out of the Components they imported from a neighboring planet. They used the last of their Components to implement their stolid metaphysic of dissection and pushing. They pushed their planet.

They knew where to push it.

Each Pyramid as it stood was a radio-astronomy observatory powerful and accurate beyond the wildest dreams of Earthly radio-astronomers. From this start, they built instruments to aid their naked senses. They went into a kind of hibernation, reducing their activity to a bare trickle except for a small "crew," and headed for the star. They had every reason to believe they would find more Components there, and they did.

Tropile was one of the newest of them, and the only thing which set him apart from the others was that he was the most recent to be stockpiled.

The religion, or vice, or philosophy he practiced made it possible for him to be a Component. Meditation derived from Zen Buddhism was a windfall for the Pyramids, though of course they had no idea at all of what lay behind it, and of course they did not "care." They knew only that at certain times certain potential Components became Components which were no longer merely potential—which were, in fact, ripe for harvesting. It was useful to them that the minds they cropped be utterly blank—it saved the step of blanking them.

Tropile had been harvested at the moment his inhibiting conscious mind had been cleared, for the Pyramids were not interested in him as an entity capable of will and conception. They used only the raw capacity of the human brain and its perceptors. They used Rashevsky's Number, the gigantic, far more than astronomical, expression that denoted the number of switching operations performable within the human brain. They used "subception," the phenome-

non by which the human mind, uninhibited
by consciousness, reacts directly to stimuli—
shortcutting the cerebral censor, avoiding the
weighing of shall-I-or-shan't-I that precedes
every conscious act.

They were—Components. It is not desir-
able that your bedroom wall switch have a
mind of its own; if you turn the lights on, you
want them *on*. So it was with the Pyramids.

A Component was needed in the industrial
complex which transforms catabolism products
into anabolism products.

With long experience gained since their
planetfall, Pyramids received the *tabula rasa*
that was Glenn Tropile. He arrived in one
piece, wearing a blanket of air. Quick-frozen
mentally at the moment of inert blankness his
meditation had granted him—the psychic
drunkard's coma—he was cushioned on repellent charges as he plummeted down, and instantly stripped of surplus electrostatic charge.

At this point he was still human; only asleep.

He remained "asleep." Annular fields they
used for lifting and lowering seized him and
moved him into a snug tank of nutrient fluid.
There were many such tanks, ready and waiting.

The tanks themselves could be moved, and
the one containing Glenn Tropile did move, to
a metabolism complex where there were many
other tanks, all occupied. This was a warm
room—the Pyramids had wasted no energy on
such foppish comforts in the receiving center.
In this room Glenn Tropile gradually resumed

the appearance of life. His heart once again began to beat. Faint stirrings were visible in his chest as his habit-numbed lungs attempted to breathe. Gradually the stirrings slowed and stopped; there was no need for that foppish comfort, either; the nutrient fluid supplied all.

Tropile was "wired into circuit."

The only literal wiring, at first, was a temporary one—a fine electrode aseptically introduced into the great nerve that leads to the rhinencephalon—the "smell brain," the area of the brain containing the pleasure centers which motivate human behavior. (More than a thousand Earthly Components had been spoiled and discarded before the Pyramids had located the pleasure centers so exactly.) While the Component Tropile was being "programmed" the wire rewarded him with minute pulses that made his body glow with animal satisfaction when he functioned correctly. That was all there was to it. After a time the wire was withdrawn, but by then Tropile had "learned" his entire task. Conditioned reflexes had been established. They could be counted on for the long and useful life of the Component.

That life might be very long indeed; in the nutrient tank beside Tropile's, as it happened, lay a Component with eight legs and a chitinous fringe around its eyes. It had lain in such a tank for more than a hundred and twenty-five thousand Terrestrial years.

*   *   *

The Component was then placed in operation. It opened its eyes and saw things; the sensory nerves of its limbs felt things; the muscles of its hands and toes operated things.

Where was Glenn Tropile?

He was there, all of him; but a zombie-Tropile. Bereft of will, emptied of memories. He was a machine and part of a huger machine. His sex was the sex of a photoelectric cell; his politics were those of a transistor; his ambition that of a mercury switch. He didn't know anything about sex, or fear, or hope. He only knew two things: Input and Output.

Input to him was a display of small lights on a board before his vacant face; and also the modulation of a loudspeaker's liquid-born hum in each ear, certain flavors, many twinges of pressure, heat or pain.

Output from him was the dancing manipulation of certain buttons and keys, prompted by changes in Input and by nothing else.

Between Input and Output he lay in the tank, Glenn Tropile, a human Black Box which was capable of Rashevsky's Number of switchings, and of nothing else.

He had been programmed to accomplish a specific task—to shepherd a chemical called 3, 7, 12-trihydroxycholanic acid, present in the catabolic product of the Pyramids, through a succession of more than five hundred separate operations until it emerged as the chemical, which the Pyramids were able to metabolize, called Protoporphin IX.

He was not the only Component operating

in this task; there were several, each with its own program. The acid accumulated in great tanks a mile from him. He knew its concentration, heat and pressure; he knew of all the impurities which would affect subsequent reactions. His fingers tapped, giving binary-coded signals to sluice gates to open for so many seconds and then to close; for such an amount of solvent at such a temperature to flow in; for the agitators to agitate for just so long at just such a force. And if a trouble signal disturbed any one of the 517 major and minor operations, he—it?—was set to decide among alternatives:

—scrap the batch in view of flow conditions along the line?

—isolate and bypass the batch through a standby loop?

—immediate action to correct the malfunction?

Without inhibiting intelligence, without the trammels of humanity on him, the intricate display board and the complex modulations of the input signals could be instantly taken in, evaluated and given their share in the decision.

Was it—he?—still alive?

The question has no meaning. It was working. It was an excellent machine, in fact, and the Pyramids cared for it well. Its only consciousness, apart from the reflexive responses that were its program, was "the sound of one hand alone": zero, mindlessness, Samadhi, stupor.

It continued to function for some time—until

the required supply of Protoporphin IX had been exceeded by a sufficient factor of safety to make further processing unnecessary—that is, for some minutes or months. During that time it was Happy. (It had been programmed to be Happy when there were no uncorrected malfunctions of the process.) At the end of that time it shut itself off, sent out a signal that the task was completed; and was then laid aside in the analogue of a deep-freeze, to be reprogrammed when another Component was needed.

No. It was of utterly no importance to the Pyramids that this particular Component had not been stamped from Citizen but from Wolf.

9

Roget Germyn, of Wheeling a Citizen, found himself thinking of Glenn Tropile much more than he would have liked.

It was not seemly for a Citizen's thoughts to keep flashing back to a cried-upon Wolf. It wasn't even sense. At this time of all times he should have devoted a seemly proportion of his thoughts—actually, nearly all of them—to his work, for this was the time when Germyn's occupation of banker was both very demanding and very enjoyable.

It was always that way in the first weeks after the birth of a New Sun. It was the time when even the soberest Citizen might permit himself to dream largely. Six months from now, when the first big harvests were already in and the earliest of the second ripening for the granaries, that was the time when a banker needed to be extremely conservative. Saving was the order of the day then. So Germyn would delicately remind his clients, deferentially counseling them to put away rather than spend, borrow only if they must, save, save, for the hard times that surely lay ahead.

Then the hard times would begin to come.

The crops would dwindle. Then Germyn would have to try harder than ever to find the words, the properly indirect and mannerly words, to keep his investors from drawing on their hoard before they had to.

Then the Old Sun would begin to die, and the harvests went from slim to zero. That was the long-drawn-out time when everyone's savings melted slowly away. Stretch it out if you can, he would say—as persuasively as a proper Citizen could. Make it last. Always keep a reserve in your account—for if you spend too much too fast, not only will you risk running out of reserves before the Re-Creation of the Sun, but you will perhaps drive up prices, and then everyone will suffer.

And then the New Sun would be born, and the world would bloom again. Like now. And if Germyn had done his work well, his bank would still have funds on deposit to make loans—to finance new ventures—to plant more farmland—to *hope*.

It was the best time of year for bankers, as well as for everyone else. It was the only time when anyone dared hope at all.

So when Germyn came home one night, he was vastly pleased with his work and his world. He was mulling over the words of mild exultation with which to share his pleasure with his wife when he opened the door.

The exultation did not last.

He contemplated his wife from behind his hand, unwilling to believe what reason and evidence told him was true.

Possibly the events of the past few days had unhinged her reason, but he was nearly sure that she had eaten a portion of the evening meal secretly, in the serving room, before calling him to table.

He felt sure that it was only a temporary aberration; she was, after all, a Citizeness, with all that that implied. A—a creature, like that Gala Tropile for example, someone like that might steal extra portions with craft and guile. You couldn't live with a Wolf for years and not have some of it rub off on you. But not Citizeness Germyn.

There was a light thrice-repeated tap on the door.

Speak of the devil, thought Roget Germyn most appropriately; for it was that same Gala Tropile. She entered, her head downcast, looking dark and haggard and—well, pretty.

He began formally, "I give you greeting, Citi—"

"They're here!" she interrupted in desperate haste. Germyn blinked. "Please," she begged, "can't you do something? They're *Wolves!*"

Citizeness Germyn emitted a muted shriek.

"You may leave, Citizeness," Germyn told her shortly, already forming in his mind the

words of gentle reproof he would later use.
"Now, what is all this talk of Wolves?" He
realized with a pang that his words were almost as gracelessly direct as her own. So completely had his wife and Tropile's erased the
sweetness of his day at the bank.

Gala Tropile distractedly sat down in the
chair her hostess had vacated. (Sat without
being invited! Not even in a guest chair! How
far gone the woman was!) "Glenn and I ran
away from you," she began drearily, "after—
you know—after he decided he didn't want to
make his Donation? After he escaped from the
House of the Five Regulations? Anyway, we
ran as far as we could, because Glenn said
there was no reason he should just sit still and
let you all murder him just because he helped
himself to a few things." Germyn was shud-
dering as he listened to that tale of horrors,
but what she said next made him sit straight
up in shock. "And then—you won't believe
this, Citizen Germyn—and then, when we
stopped to rest, a day's march away, an aircraft came!"

Citizen Germyn didn't. "An aircraft!" He
allowed himself a frown. "Citizeness, it is not
well to say things which are not so."

"I saw it, Citizen! There were men in it,
and one of them is here again. He came looking for me with another man, and I barely
escaped him. I'm afraid!"

"There is no cause for fear, only an opportunity to appreciate," Citizen Germyn said
mechanically—it was what you told your chil-

dren. But within himself, he was finding it very hard to remain calm. That word, Wolf—it was a destroyer of calm, it was an incitement to panic and hatred! He remembered Tropile well, and there was Wolf, to be sure. The mere fact that Citizen Germyn had doubted his Wolfishness at first was now powerful cause to be doubly convinced of it; he had postponed the day of reckoning for an enemy of all the world, and there was enough secret guilt in his recollection to set his own heart thumping.

"Tell me exactly what happened," said Citizen Germyn, in words that the stress of emotion had already made far less than graceful.

Obediently Gala Tropile said: "I was returning to my home after the evening meal and Citizeness Puffin—she took me in after Citizen Tropile—after my husband was—"

"I understand. You made your home with her."

"Yes. She told me that two men had come to see me. They spoke badly, she said, and I was alarmed. I peered through a window of my own home, and they were there. One had been in the aircraft I saw! And they flew away with my husband."

"It is a matter of seriousness," Citizen Germyn admitted doubtfully. "So that then you came to me?"

"Yes, but they saw me, Citizen! And I think they followed. You must protect me, I have no one else!"

"If they be Wolf," Germyn said calmly, "we

will raise hue and cry against them. Now, will the Citizeness remain here? I go forth to see these men."

There was a graceless hammering on the door.

"Too late!" cried Gala Tropile in panic. "They are here!"

Citizen Germyn went through the ritual of greeting, of deprecating the ugliness and poverty of his home, of offering everything he owned to his visitors; it was the way to greet a stranger.

The two men lacked both courtesy and wit; but they did make an attempt to comply with the minimal formal customs of introduction. He had to give them credit for that; and yet it was almost more alarming than if they had blustered and yelled.

For he knew one of these men.

He dredged the name out of his memory. It was Haendl. This man appeared in Wheeling the day Glenn Tropile had been scheduled to make the Donation of the Spinal Tap and had broken free and escaped. He had inquired about Tropile of a good many people, Citizen Germyn included; and even at that time, in the excitement of an Amok, a Wolf-finding and a Translation in a single day, Germyn had wondered at his lack of breeding and airs.

Now he wondered no longer.

But the man made no such overt act as Tropile's terrible theft of bread, and Citizen Germyn postponed the raising of the hue and cry. It was not a thing to be undertaken lightly.

"Gala Tropile is in this house," the man with Haendl said bluntly.

Citizen Germyn managed a Quirked Smile.

"We want to see her, Germyn. It's about her husband. He—uh, he was with us for a while and something happened."

"Ah, yes. The Wolf."

The man flushed and looked at Haendl. Haendl said loudly: "The Wolf. Sure he's a Wolf. But he's gone now, so you don't have to worry about that."

"Gone?"

Haendl said angrily: "Not just him, but four or five of us. There was a man named Innison, and he's gone too. We need help, Germyn. Something about Tropile—God knows how it is, but he started something. We want to talk to his wife and find out what we can about him. So will you get her out of the back room where she's hiding and bring her here, please?"

Citizen Germyn quivered. He vent over the ID bracelet that once had belonged to the late PFC Joe Hartmann, fingering it to hide his thoughts. He said at last: "Perhaps you are right. Perhaps the Citizeness is with my wife. If this were so, would it not be possible that she was fearful of those who once were with her husband?"

Haendl laughed sourly. "She isn't any more fearful than we are, Germyn. Let me tell you something. I told you about this man Innison who disappeared. He was a Son of the Wolf, you understand me? For that matter—" He glanced at his companion, licked his lips and changed his mind about what he had been going to say next. "He was a Wolf. Do you ever remember hearing of a Wolf being Translated before?"

"Translated?" Germyn dropped the ID bracelet. "But that's impossible!" he cried, forgetting his manners completely. "Oh, no. Translation comes only to those who attain the moment of supreme detachment, you can be sure of that. I know. I've seen it with my own eyes. No Wolf could *possibly*—"

"At least five Wolves did," Haendl said grimly. "Now you see what the trouble is? Tropile was Translated—I saw that with *my* own eyes. The next day, Innison. Within a week, two or three others. So we came down here, Germyn, not because we like you people, not because we enjoy it. But because we're *scared*. What we want is to talk to Tropile's wife—you too, I guess; we want to talk to anybody who ever knew him. We want to find out everything there is to find out about Tropile, and see if we can make any sense of the answers. Because maybe Translation is the supreme objective of life to you people, Germyn, but to us it's just one more way of dying. And we don't want to die."

Citizen Germyn bent to pick up his cherished identification bracelet and dropped it absently on a table. There was very much on his mind.

He said at last: "That is strange. Shall I tell you another strange thing?"

Haendl, looking angry and baffled, nodded.

Germyn said: "There has been no Translation here since the day the Wolf, Tropile, escaped. But there have been Eyes. I have seen them myself. It—" he hesitated, and shrugged—"it has been disturbing. Some of our finest Citizens have ceased to Meditate; they have been worrying. So many Eyes, and no one taken! It is outside of all of our experience, and our customs have suffered. Politeness is dwindling among us; even in my own household—"

He coughed and went on: "No matter. But these Eyes have come into every home; they have peered about, peered about, and no one has been taken. Why? Is it something to do with the Translation of Wolves?" He stared hopelessly at his visitors. "All I know," he said, "is that it is very strange, and therefore I am worried."

Haendl boomed: "Then take us to Gala Tropile. Let's see what we can find out!"

Citizen Germyn bowed. He cleared his throat and raised his voice just sufficiently to carry from one room to another. "Citizeness!" he called.

There was a pause and then his wife appeared in the doorway, looking concerned.

"Will you ask if Citizeness Tropile will join us here?" he requested.

His wife nodded. "She is resting. I will suggest to her that it would be pleasant to speak together. . . ."

But that Citizeness Germyn did not do.

As she turned, there was a sound of two hands loudly clapping from the other room.

All four of them jumped, and stared. Then the nearly self-admitted Wolf, Haendl, ran for the door and the others followed.

The thunderclap had been real, though not of any human hands. Air had rushed in to fill a void. The void had been the volume of space that once had been occupied by Citizeness Gala Tropile.

Roget Germyn turned pale. This woman— this Wolf-tainted woman, surely in no state for the grace of meditation—she had been Translated, too!

10

On the binary planet, the former Wolf (and also former human being) named Glenn Tropile had been reprogrammed.

In some ways, the Earth had been a disappointment to the Pyramids. True, it was wonderfully rich in Components, and the Components seemed perfectly willing to reseed and recultivate and reproduce themselves indefinitely. There were not as many as there once had been, to be sure, but you couldn't knock a wrist-watch mine that kept on generating new wrist-watches. Moreover, these particular Components were high-grade goods. They were of a usefully high order of complexity, suitable for programming into almost any area of Pyramid concern: calculation, manufacture, repair, processing, data storage, whatever. It was also true that these particular Components had the delightful habit of ripening themselves for the greatest ease of assimilation; often as not, they arrived on the binary with their minds wholly blank and ready for recording upon. (The Pyramids didn't know this was called "meditation", and of course would not have cared anyway.)

The only thing that was really wrong with Earthly Components was their unfortunate anatomy. Because they were land-dwellers, and from a planet with an undesirably high surface gravity at that, they had evolved all that completely unnecessary investment in skeletons and muscles and, of course, digestive and eliminatory systems to support them. The Pyramids liked *little* Components, with nerve-endings packed closely on the surface of their bodies and small but quick limbs (or tentacles or pseudopods).

(Of course, this was not really a problem for the Pyramids. There *were* no problems for the Pyramids. Take-apart-and-shove was good enough for them. The details they left to the million million systems and sub-systems that filled their dead old planet from crust to crust. Those systems, themselves Component-directed, were quite able to make do with odd-shaped Components, though it did involve a certain amount of rearranging—surgical, for example.)

So the Pyramids dragged their captive planet out of the Earth's solar system, questing after that dream, the planet of perfect Components. Like any prudent traveler, they took the Earth as a sort of picnic lunch to sustain them on the way. They were not tidy picnickers. They had strewn half the Galaxy with the discards of earlier journeys. Some day, no doubt, they would have consumed all they wanted from the tuck basket that was the Earth. Then they would simply let go of it. There would be no further Re-Creation of the Sun. In only a wink of time—a few decades at the most—the planet would radiate the last of its stored heat, and drift frozen for all the rest of eternity.

But that moment was not yet.

Now it was the time for navigation. The Pyramids had taken Earth out past the orbit of Pluto with a simple shove, slow and massive. It had been enough merely to approximate the direction in which, eventually, they would want to go. There would be plenty of time for refining the course later, once the spiral had opened almost to a straight line.

The systems concerned with such things as navigation knew where they were going, at least in general terms. There was a star-cluster reasonably sure to be rich in Componentiferous planets. It was inherent in the nature of Component mines that eventually they played out. They had always done so.

That didn't matter. There were always more mines. If that had not been so it would have been necessary, perhaps, to stockpile Components against future needs. But things being as they were, it was easier to work the vein out and move on.

This next hop would be quite a short one for the Pyramids, no more than a couple of thousand years at the maximum. Nevertheless, the navigation should be carefully done. Many of the navigation systems had been unused for a long time. Some of them were no longer functioning at optimum levels, because Components had failed. (It was the nature of Components to fail after a while. The Pyramids knew this, though they themselves were made to last forever; they accepted the fact that the life of a component was seldom more than some tens of thousands of years.) Other systems needed new data, small-scale information but important, on regions of the Galaxy not studied before.

This was all old stuff to the Pyramids. They knew how to handle it. They broke the subject down to its essentials, separated even those into component parts. One set of systems opened great telescopic eyes in all frequencies to gaze at the astronomical objects before them. Others began the endless series of parallel-processed calculations that determined where to shove, and how hard. Maintenance systems within all of the others performed check-tests and identified Components that needed to be replaced.

When they found a defective Component—human, reptile, protozoan, plant or whatever—they turfed it out and replaced it with a fresh one out of stores. The used Components weren't wasted. They simply became soup stock for feeding the ones that were still in working order.

This reinforced the chronic need for new Components. Therefore some stand-by Component-seeking systems were reactivated, by supplying them, of course, with new Components. Finding new components (by issuing appropriate instructions to the single Pyramid on Earth's Mount Everest) was itself far too complex for a single component, but the Pyramids knew how to handle it. They broke the problem down to its essentials; separated even those into many parts. There was, for example, the subsection of one certain aspect of the logistic problem involved which involved locating and procuring additional Components to handle the load.

Even that tiny specialization was too much for a single Component, but the Pyramids had resources to bring to bear. The procedure in such cases was to hitch several Components together.

This was done.

When the Pyramids finished their neuro-surgery, there floated in an oversized nutrient tank a thing like a great sea-anemone. It was composed of eight Components—all human, as it happened—arranged in a circle, facing inward, joined temple to temple, brain to brain.

At their feet, where sixteen eyes could see it, was the display board to feed them their visual Input. Sixteen hands grasped each a moulded switch to handle their binary-coded Output. There would be no storage of the Output outside of the eight-Component complex itself; it went as control signals to the electrostatic generators, funneled through the single Pyramid on Mount Everest, which handled the task of Component-procurement.

That is, of Translation.

The programming was slow and thorough. Perhaps the Pyramid which finally activated the octuple unit and went away was pleased with itself, not knowing that one of its Components was Glenn Tropile.

Nirvana. (It pervaded all; there was nothing outside of it.)

Nirvana. (Glenn Tropile floated in it as in the amniotic fluid around him.)

Nirvana . . . The sound of one hand . . . Floating one-ness . . .

There was an intrusion.

Perfection is complete; by adding to it, it is destroyed. *Duality struck like a thunderbolt. One-ness shattered.*

For Glenn Tropile, it seemed as though his wife were screaming at him to wake up. He tried.

It was curiously difficult and painful. Timeless poignant sadness, five years of sorrow over a lost love compressed into a microsecond. It was always so, Tropile thought drowsily, awakening; it never lasts; what's the use of worrying over what always happens. . . .

Sudden shock and horror rocked him.

This was no ordinary awakening. No ordinary thing at all, *nothing* was as it ever had been before!

Tropile opened his mouth and screamed—or thought he did. But there was only a hoarse, faint flutter in his eardrums.

It was a moment when sanity might have

gone. But there was one curious, mundane fact that saved him. He was holding something in his hands. He found that he could look at it, and it was a switch. A moulded switch, mounted on a board; and he was holding one in each hand.

It was little to cling to, but it at least was real. If his hands could be holding something, then there must be some reality somewhere.

Tropile closed his eyes and managed to open them again. Yes, there was reality too; he closed his eyes and light stopped; he opened them and light returned.

Then perhaps he was not dead, as he had thought.

Carefully, stumblingly—his mind his only usable tool—he tried to make an estimate of his surroundings. He could hardly believe what he found.

Item, he could scarcely move. Somehow he was bound by his feet and his head. How? He couldn't tell.

Item, he was bent over and he couldn't straighten. Why? Again he couldn't tell, but it was a fact. The great extensor muscles of his back answered his command, but his body would not move.

Item, his eyes saw, but only in a small area.

He couldn't move his head, either. Still, he could see a few things. The switches in his hands, his feet, a sort of display of lights on a strange circular board.

The lights flickered and changed their pattern.

Without thinking, he clicked the lefthand switch:— Why? Because it was *right* to do so. When a certain light flared green, a certain sequence had to be clicked. Why, again? Well, when a certain light flared green, a certain sequence—

He abandoned that problem. Never mind why; what the devil was going *on?*

Glenn Tropile squinted about him like a mollusc peering out of its shell. There was another fact, the oddness of the seeing. What makes it look so queer? he asked himself.

He found an answer, but it required some time to take it in. He was seeing in a strange perspective. One looks out of two eyes. Close one eye and the world is flat. Open it again, and there is a stereoscopic double; the saliencies of the picture leap forward, the background retreats.

So with the lights on the board—no, not exactly; but something *like* that, he thought. It was as though—he squinted and strained—as though he had never really *seen* before. As though for all his life he had had only one eye, and now he had strangely been given two.

His visual perception of the board was *total*. He could see all of it at once. It had no "front" or "back;" it was in the round; the natural thinking of it was without orientation; he engulfed and comprehended it as a unit. It had no secrets of shadow or silhouette.

I think, Tropile mouthed slowly to himself, I think I'm going crazy.

But that was no explanation either. Mere insanity didn't account for what he saw.

Then, he asked himself, was he in a state that was *beyond* Nirvana? He remembered, with an odd flash of guilt, that he had been meditating; watching the stages of boiling water. All right, perhaps he had been Translated. But what was this, then? Were the meditators wrong in teaching that Nirvana was the end—and yet righter than the Wolves, who dismissed Meditation as a phenomenon wholly inside the skull, and refused to discuss Translation at all?

That was a question for which he could find nothing approaching an answer. He turned away from it and looked at his hands.

He could see them, too, in the round, he noted; he could see every wrinkle and pore in all sixteen of them. . . .

Sixteen hands!

That was the other moment when sanity might have gone.

He closed his eyes. (Sixteen eyes! No wonder the total perception!) And after a while he opened them again.

The hands were there. All sixteen of them.

Cautiously, Tropile selected a finger that seemed familiar in his memory and, after a moment's thought, flexed it. It bent. He selected another. Another—on a different hand, this time.

He could use any or all of the sixteen hands. They were all his, all sixteen of them.

I appear, thought Tropile crazily, to be a sort of eight-branched snowflake. Each of my branches is a human body.

He stirred, and added another datum. I appear also to be in a tank of fluid, and yet I do not drown.

There were certain deductions to be made from that. Either someone—the Pyramids?—had done something to his lungs, or else the fluid was as good an oxygenating medium as air. Or both.

Suddenly a burst of data-lights twinkled on the board below him. Instantly and involuntarily, his sixteen hands began working the switches, transmitting complex directions in a lightning-like stream of on-off clicks.

Tropile relaxed and let it happen. He had no choice; the power that made it *right* to respond to the board made it impossible for his brain to concentrate while the response was going on. Perhaps, he thought drowsily, perhaps he would never have awakened at all if it had not been for the long period with no lights. . . .

But he was awake. And his consciousness began to explore as the task ended.

He had had an opportunity to understand something of what was happening. He understood that he was now a part of something larger than himself, beyond doubt something which served and belonged to the Pyramids. His single brain not being large enough for the job, seven others had been hooked in with it.

But where were their personalities?

Gone, he supposed; presumably, they had been Citizens. Sons of the Wolf did not meditate, and therefore were not Translated—except for himself, he added wryly, remembering the meditation on Rainclouds that had led him to—

No, wait! Not Rainclouds but Water!

Tropile caught hold of himself and forced his mind to retrace that thought. He *remembered* the Raincloud Meditation. It had been prompted by a particularly noble cumulus of the Ancient Ship type.

And this was odd. Tropile had never been deeply interested in Rainclouds; had never known even the secondary classifications of Raincloud types. And he *knew* that the Ancient Ship variety was of the fourth order of categories.

It was a false memory. *It was not his.*

Therefore, logically, it was someone else's memory; and being available to his own mind, as the fourteen other hands and eyes were available, it must belong to—another branch of the snowflake.

He turned his eyes down and tried to see which of the branches was his old body. He found it quickly, with growing excitement. There was the left great toe of his own body, a deformed blade twice as thick as it should be; he had injured it in boyhood, it had come off and grown back wrong. Good! It was reassuring.

He tried to feel the one particular body that led to that familiar toe.

He succeeded, not easily. After a time he became more aware of *that* body—somewhat as a neurotic may become "stomach conscious" or "heart conscious;" but this was no neurosis, it was an intentional exploration.

Since that worked, with some uneasiness he transferred his attention to another pair of feet and "thought" his way up from them.

It was embarrassing.

For the first time in his life he knew what it felt like to have breasts. For the first time in his life he knew what it was like to have one's internal organs quite differently shaped and arranged, buttressed and stressed by different muscles. The very faint background feel of man's internal arrangements, never questioned unless something goes wrong with them and they start to hurt, was not at all like the faint background feel that a woman has inside her.

And when he concentrated on that feel, it was no faint background to him. It was surprising and upsetting.

He withdrew his attention—hoping that he would be able to. He was. Gratefully he became conscious of his own body again. Somehow, he was still *himself* if he chose to be.

Were the other seven?

He reached into his mind—*all* of it, all eight separate intelligences that were combined within him.

"Is anybody there?" he demanded.

No answer—or nothing he could recognize as an answer. He drove harder, and there was still no answer. It was annoying. He resented it as bitterly, he remembered, as in the old days when he had first been learning the subtleties of Raincloud Appreciation. There had been a Raincloud Master, his name forgotten, who had been sometimes less than courteous, had driven hard—

Another false memory!

He withdrew and weighed it. Perhaps, he thought, that was a part of the answer. These people, these other seven, would not be driven. The attempt to call them back to consciousness would have to be delicate. When he drove hard it was painful—he remembered the instant violent agony of his own awakening—and they reacted with unhappiness.

More gently, alert for vagrant "memories," he combed the depths of the eightfold mind within him, reaching into the sleeping portions, touching, handling, sifting and associating, sorting. This memory of an old knife wound from an Amok—that was not the Raincloud woman; it was a man, very aged. This faint recollection of a childhood fear of drowning— was that she? It was; it fitted with this other recollection, the long detour on the road south toward the sun, around a river.

The Raincloud woman was the first to round out in his mind, and the first he communicated with. He was not surprised to find that, early in her life, she had feared that she might be Wolf.

He reached out for her. It was almost magic—knowing the "secret name" of a person, so that then he was yours to command. But the "secret name" was more than that; it was the gestalt of the person; it was the sum of all data and experience, never available to another person—until now.

With her memories arranged at last in his own mind, he thought persuasively: "Citizeness Alla Narova, will you awaken and speak with me?"

No answer—only a vague, troubled stirring.

Gently he persisted: "I know you well, Alla Narova. You sometimes thought you might be a Daughter of the Wolf, but never really believed it because you knew you loved your husband—and thought Wolves did not love. You loved Rainclouds, too. It was when you stood at Beachy Head and saw a great cumulus that you went into meditation—"

And on and on.

He repeated himself many times, coaxingly. Even so it was not easy; but at last he began to reach into her. Slowly she began to surface. Thoughts faintly sounded in his mind. Like echoes, at first; his own thoughts bouncing back at him; a sort of mental nod of agreement, "Yes, that is so." Then—terror. A shaking fear; a hysterical rush; Citizeness Alla Narova came violently up to full consciousness and to panic.

She was soundlessly screaming. The whole eight-branched figure quivered and twisted in its nutrient bath.

The terrible storm raged in Tropile's own mind as fully as in hers—but he had the ad-

vantage of knowing what it was. He helped
her. He fought it for the two of them . . .
soothing, explaining, calming.

He won.

At last her branch of the snowflake-body
retreated, sobbing for a spell. The storm was
over.

He talked to her in his mind and she "listened." She was incredulous, but there was no
choice for her; she *had* to believe.

Exhausted and passive she asked finally:
"What can we do? I wish I were dead!"

He told her: "You never were such a cow-
ard before. Remember, Alla Narova, I *know*
you."

The thought returned from her: "And I know
you. As nobody has ever known another human being before."

Then they were thinking together, inextri-
cably: More than conversation. More than
communion. More than love. Remember how
you feared defloration? I remember. And you,
with your fear of impotence on the wedding
night! I remember. Must we be indecent to
each other? I think we must. After all, you're
the first man who ever had a baby. And you're
the first woman who ever sired one. Past
shame, past shyness, into a pool of ourselves.

Tropile's hands clicked codes as the display
lights shifted. It was so damned queer. He
was he and she was she and together they
were—what? She was good and kind or he
might not have been able to bear it. She had
sheltered that poor blind man in Cadiz for a

year; during the crop failure at Vincennes she had bravely gone into the fields and done unwomanly work for all; she had murdered her husband in a fit of rage, a short and secret amok—

"Get away from me!" he screamed. It was all there in his memory. A scuffed glass paperweight, very ancient and the size of a man's fist, with swirling streaks of color in it, dim under the hundred nicks and chips on the surface, and an inset square plate of porcelain that said in ornamental Wedgwood blue letters GOD BLESS OUR HOME. His husband had laid there snoring and the snow had begun sifting down outside the tent wall, and she had battered, and battered mercilessly, red-eyed and hissing, consumed with hate and blood lust. She had done it; how could he forget the bubbling horror of the face that kept living and sputtering after the eyes had been bashed sightless and the jaw hung smashed in eight places, limber as the backbone of a snake?

"Get away from me!" he screamed.

She said only: "How?"

He began to laugh, titteringly. Perhaps if he laughed this twinness with a monster would not seem so bad. The whole thing was probably some universal joke of which he had just seen the point; he would spend the rest of his life laughing.

"Pervert," she said to him. "Yes, I killed my husband, and you perverted your wife, giving her what she felt was a small living death, turning her love into sickness and shame. I suppose we are well matched. I can live with you, pervert."

It came through; it was not part of the joke. "And I can live with you, murderess," he said at last. "Because I know you're not just murderess. There was Cadiz and Vincennes, too."

"And for you there were a hundred daily tendernesses you gave your wife to compensate for evil. You are not so bad, Tropile. You are a human being."

"And so are you. But what are—we?"

"We must begin to find out. It is all so new. We must try to trick ourselves into finding out what we are, otherwise you and I will always stand in the way of Us."

Tropile said: "If I told a story it would be about the famous Captain Sir Roderick Flandray, Intelligence Corps, Imperial Terran Space Navy—dark, sardonic, bright with melancholy, quite impossible, my asinine ideal."

"And my story would be about doomed Iseult who flung herself from life into love like a rock-fanged Cornish coast, the poor fool. Farewell to the pleasures of the table and the stool; the world well lost for a few overrated contractions. But that is what my story would be about; I cannot help being what I am."

They laughed together, and together went on: "If *we* told a story it would be about a circular fire that grew."

And they jerked back in an ecstasy of terror at what they had said.

They were silent for a long time while their hands clicked and clicked away at the switches.

"I want no more of that," Alla Narova said finally. "Or—?" She did not know.

"I have never been so frightened in my life," Glenn Tropile said, "nor have you. Nor have we ever been so tantalized by a hint of meaning. *My* hero is Lucifer; *your* heroine is Ishtar the Young. *Ours* is a circular fire that grows."

They were silent for a time, while Tropile pondered this new self with its new vocabulary and new memories. Was he still Glenn Tropile at all?

It didn't seem to matter.

Many clicks later, Alla Narova said wistfully, "Of course, there is nothing we can *do*."

Wolf rose in the heart of the Component named Glenn Tropile. "Don't say that," Tropile cried, astonished at his own fury.

Diplomatically, she said, "Yes, but really—"

"Really," he said with a savage bite, "there's always something. We just don't know what it is."

Another long silence, and then Alla Narova said, "I wonder if we can wake the others."

11

Haendl was on the ragged edge of a nervous breakdown. It was something new in his life.

It was full hot summer, and the hidden colony of Wolves in Princeton should have been full of energy and life. The crops were growing on all the fields nearby; the drained storehouses were being replenished. The aircraft that had been so painfully rebuilt and fitted for the assault on Mount Everest were standing by, ready to be manned and to take off.

And nothing, absolutely nothing, was going right.

It looked as though there would *be* no expedition to Everest. Four times now Haendl had gathered his forces and been all ready. Four times a key man of the expedition had—vanished.

Wolves didn't vanish!

And yet more than a score of them had.

First Tropile—then Innison—then two dozen more, by ones and twos; no one was immune. Take Innison, for example. There was a man who was Wolf through and through. He was a doer, not a thinker; his skills were the skills of an artisan, a tinkerer, a jackleg mechanic. How could a man like that succumb to the pallid lure of meditation?

But undeniably he had. Translated. Gone!

It had reached a point where Haendl himself was red-eyed and fretful. He had set curious alarms for himself—had enlisted the help of others of the colony to avert the danger of Translation from himself. When he went to bed at night, a lieutenant sat next to his bed, watchfully alert lest Haendl, in that moment of reverie before sleep, fall into meditation—and himself be Translated. There was no hour of the day when Haendl permitted himself to be alone; and his companions, or guards, were ordered to shake him awake, as violently as need be, at the first hint of an abstracted look in the eyes or a reflective cast of the features. As time went on, Haendl's self-imposed regime of constant alertness began to cost him heavily in lost rest and sleep. And the consequences of that were: More and more occasions when the bodyguards shook him awake; less and less rest.

He was very close to breakdown indeed.

On a hot, wet morning a few days after his useless expedition to see Citizen Germyn in Wheeling, Haendl ate a tasteless breakfast and, reeling with fatigue, set out on a tour of inspection of Princeton. Warm rain dripped from low clouds; but that was merely one more annoyance to Haendl. He hardly noticed it.

There were upwards of a thousand Wolves in the Community; and there were signs of worry on the face of every one of them. Haendl was not the only man in Princeton who had begun laying traps for himself as a result of the unprecedented disappearances; he was not the only one who was short of sleep. A community of a thousand is closeknit. When one member in forty disappears, the morale of the whole community receives a shattering blow. To Haendl it was clear, looking into the faces of his compatriots, that not only was it going to be nearly impossible to mount the planned assault on the Pyramid on Everest this year, it was going to be unbearably difficult merely to keep the community going.

The whole Wolf pack was on the verge of panic.

There was a confused shouting behind Haendl. Groggily he turned and looked; half a dozen Wolves were yelling and pointing at something in the wet, muggy air.

It was an Eye, hanging silent and featureless over the center of the street.

Haendl took a deep breath and mustered command of himself. "Frampton!" he ordered one of his lieutenants. "Get the helicopter with the instruments here. We'll get some more readings."

Frampton opened his mouth, then looked more closely at Haendl and, instead, began to

talk on his pocket radio. Haendl knew what
was in the man's mind—it was in his own, too.
What was the use of more readings? From the
time of Tropile's Translation on, they had had
a perfect superfluity of instrument readings on
the forces and auras that surrounded the Eyes—
yes, and on Translations themselves, too. Before Tropile there had never been an Eye
seen in Princeton, much less an actual Translation; but things were different now, everything was different; Eyes roamed restlessly
around day and night.

Some of the men nearest the Eye were
picking up rocks and clods of dirt and throwing them at the bobbing vortex in the air.
Haendl started to yell at them to stop, then
changed his mind. The Eye didn't seem to be
affected—as he watched, one of the men scored
a direct hit with a cobblestone. The stone
went right through the Eye, without sound or
effect; why not let them work off some of their
fears in direct action?

There was a fluttering of helicopter vanes,
and the copter with the instruments mounted
on it came down in the middle of the street,
between Haendl and the Eye.

It was all very rapid from then on in.

The Eye swooped toward Haendl. He
couldn't help it; he ducked. That was useless,
beyond doubt; but it was also unnecessary, for
he saw in a second that it was only partly the
motion of the Eye toward him that made it
loom larger; it was also that the Eye itself was
growing. An Eye was perhaps the size of a

football, as near as anyone could judge; this one got bigger, bigger; it was the size of a roc's egg, the size of a whale's blunt head. It stopped and hovered over the helicopter, while the man inside frantically pointed lenses and meters—

Thundercrash.

Not a man this time; Translation had gone beyond men; the whole helicopter vanished, man, instruments, spinning vanes and all.

Haendl picked himself up, sweating, shocked beyond sleepiness.

The young man named Frampton said fearfully, "Haendl, what do we do now?"

"Do?" Haendl stared at him absently. "Why, kill ourselves, I guess." He nodded soberly, as though he had at last attained the solution of a difficult problem. Then he sighed. "Well, one thing before that," he said. "I'm going to Wheeling. We Wolves are licked; maybe the Citizens can help us now."

Roget Germyn, of Wheeling a Citizen, received the message in the chambers that served him as a place of business. He had a visitor waiting for him at home.

Germyn was still Citizen, and he could not break off the pleasant and interminable discussion he was having with a prospective client over a potential business arrangement—not rapidly. He apologized for the interruption caused by the message the conventional three times, listened while his guest explained the plan he had come to propose in full once more, then turned his cupped hands toward himself in the gesture of denial of adequacy. It was the closest he could come to saying no.

On the other side of the desk, the Citizen who had come to propose an investment scheme immediately changed the subject by inviting Germyn and his Citizeness to a Sirius-Viewing, the invitation in the form of rhymed couplets. He had wanted to transact his business very much, but he couldn't *insist*.

Germyn got out of the invitation by a Conditional Acceptance in proper form, and the man left, delayed only slightly by the Four Urgings to stay. Almost immediately Germyn dismissed his clerk and closed his office for the day by tying a complex triple knot in a length of red cord across the open door.

When he got to his home he found, as he had suspected, that the visitor was Haendl.

There was much doubt in Citizen Germyn's mind about Haendl. The man had nearly admitted to being Wolf, and how could a Citizen overlook that? But in the excitement of Gala Tropile's Translation the matter had been less urgent than normally; there had been no hue and cry: Germyn had permitted the man to leave. And now?

He reserved judgment. He found Haendl uncomfortably sipping tea in his living room and attempting to keep up a formal conversation with Citizeness Germyn. Germyn rescued him, took him aside, closed a door—and waited.

He was astonished at the change in the

man. Before Haendl had been bouncy, aggres-
sive, quick-moving—the very qualities least
desired in a Citizen, the mark of the Son of
the Wolf. Now he was none of these things,
but he looked no more like a Citizen for all
that; he was haggard, fretful. He looked like a
man who had been through a very hard time.

He said, with an absolute minimum of pro-
tocol: "Germyn, the last time I saw you there
was a Translation. Gala Tropile, remember?"

"I remember," Citizen Germyn said eco-
nomically. Remember! It had hardly left his
thoughts.

"And you said there had been others since.
Have they still been going on?"

Germyn said: "There have." He was trying
to speak directly, to match this man Haendl's
speed and forcefulness. It was hardly good
manners, but it had occurred to Citizen Germyn that there were times when manners,
after all, were not the most important things
in the world. "There were two in the past few
days. One was a woman—Citizeness Baird;
her husband's a teacher. She was Viewing
Through Glass with four or five other women
at the time. She just—disappeared. I think
she was looking through a green prism at the
time, if that helps."

"I don't know if it helps or not. Who was
the other one?"

Germyn shrugged. "A man named Harmane.
He was our Keeper. No one saw it. But they
heard the thunderclap, or something like a
thunderclap, and he was missing." He thought

for a moment. "It is a little unusual, I suppose. Two in one week, in one little town—"

Haendl said roughly: "Listen, Germyn. It isn't just two. In the past thirty days, within the area around here and in one other place, there have been at least fifty. In two places, do you understand? Here and in Princeton. The rest of the world—no; nothing much; a few Translations here and there, but no more than usual. But just in these two communities, fifty. Does that make sense?"

Citizen Germyn thought. "—No."

"No. And I'll tell you something else. Three of the—well, victims have been children under the age of five. One was too young to walk. And the most recent Translation wasn't a person at all. It was a helicopter. Know what a helicopter is? It's a flying machine, about the size of this house. The whole damned *thing* went, bang. Now figure that out, Germyn. What's the explanation for Translations?"

Germyn was gaping. "Why—you meditate on connectivity. Once you've grasped the essential connectivity of all things, you become One with the Cosmic Whole. But I don't see how a baby—or a machine—"

"Tropile's the link," Haendl said grimly. "When he got Translated we thought it was a big help, because he had the decency to do it right under our eyes. We got enough readings to give us a clue as to what, physically speaking, Translation is all about. That was the first real clue, and we thought he'd done us a favor. . . . Now I'm not so sure." He leaned forward. "Every person I know of who was Translated was someone Tropile knew. The three kids were in his class at the nursery school—we put him onto that for a while to keep him busy, when he first came to us. Two of the men he bunked with are gone; the mess boy who served him is gone; his wife is gone. Meditation? No, Germyn. I *know* most of those people. Not a damned one of them would have spent a moment meditating on connnectivity to save his life. And what do you make of that?"

Germyn said, swallowing hard, "I just remembered. That man, Harmane—"

"What about him?"

"The one who was Translated last week. He knew Tropile too. He was the Keeper of the House of the Five Regulations when Tropile was there."

"You see? And I'll bet the woman knew him too." Haendl got up fretfully, pacing around. "Here's the thing, Germyn," he said. "I'm licked. You know what I am, don't you?"

Germyn said levelly: "I believe you to be Wolf."

"You believe right." Germyn winced in spite of himself, but managed to sit quiet and listen. "I'm telling you that doesn't matter any more. You don't like Wolves. Well, I don't like you. But this thing is too big for me to care about that any more. Tropile has started something happening, and what the end of it is going to be I can't tell. But I know this: We're not safe, either of us. Maybe you still think Translation is a fulfillment. I don't; it scares me. *But it's going to happen to me*—and to you, too. It's going to happen to everyone who ever had anything to do with Glenn Tropile. Unless we can somehow stop it—I don't know how. Will you help me?"

Germyn, trying not to tremble—when all his buried fears screamed *Wolf!*—said honestly: "I don't know if I can. I'll—I'll have to sleep on it."

Haendl looked at him for a moment. Then he shrugged. Almost to himself he said: "Maybe it doesn't matter. Maybe we can't do anything about it anyhow. All right. I'll come back in the morning, and if you've made up your mind to help, we'll start trying to make plans. And if you've made up your mind the other way— well, I'll have to fight off a few Citizens. Not that I mind that."

Germyn stood up and bowed. He began the ritual Four Urgings, but Haendl was having none of it. "Spare me that," he growled. "Meanwhile, Germyn, if I were you I wouldn't make any long-range plans. You may not be here to carry them out."

Germyn said thoughtfully: "And if you were *you*?"

"I'm not making any, either," Haendl said grimly.

Citizen Germyn, feeling utterly tainted with the scent of the Wolf in his home, tossed in his bed, sleepless. His eyes were wide open, staring at the dark ceiling. He could hear his wife's decorous breathing from the foot of the bed—soft, regular, it should have been lulling him to sleep.

It was not. Sleep was very far away.

Germyn was a brave enough man, as courage is measured among Citizens. That is to say, he had never been afraid; though it was true that there had been very little occasion. But he was afraid now. He didn't want to be Translated.

The Wolf, Haendl, had put his finger on it: *Perhaps you still think Translation is a fulfillment*. But he didn't, of course; that was riduclous now. Translation—the reward of meditation, the gift bestowed on only a handful of gloriously transfigured persons. That was one thing. But the sort of Translation that was now involved was nothing like that; not if it happened to children; not if it happened to Gala Tropile; not if it happened to a machine.

And Glenn Tropile was involved in it.

Germyn tossed and turned.

There is an ancient and infallible recipe for curing warts. Take a blade of grass, boil it in a pot of water, cool the water, soak the wart in it for nine seconds. The wart will go away— provided that during those nine seconds you do not think of the word "rhinoceros."

What was keeping Citizen Germyn awake was the attempt to *not* think of the word "rhinoceros"—or, in this case, "connectivity." It had come to him that if (a) people who knew Glenn Tropile were likely to be Translated, and (b) people who meditated on connectivity were likely to be Translated, then, a plus b, people who knew Glenn Tropile and didn't want to be Translated had better not meditate on connectivity.

It was very difficult to *not* think of connectivity.

Endlessly he calculated sums in arithmetic in his mind, recited the Five Regulations, composed Greeting Poems and Verses on Viewing. And endlessly he kept coming back to Tropile, to Translation, to connectivity. He didn't *want* to be Translated. But still the thought had a certain lure. What was it like? he wondered. Did it hurt?

Well, probably not, he speculated. It was very fast, according to Haendl's report—if you could believe what an admitted Son of the Wolf reported. But he had to, this time. Well, if it was fast—at that kind of speed, he thought, perhaps you would die instantly. Maybe Tropile was dead. Was that possible? But no, it didn't seem so; after all, there was the fact of the connection between Tropile and so many of the recently Translated. What was the connection there? Or, generalizing, what connections were involved in—

He rescued himself and summoned up the first image that came to mind. It happened to be Tropile's wife. Gala Tropile; who had disappeared herself, in this very room.

Gala Tropile. He stuck close to the thought of her, a little pleased with himself. That was the trick of *not* thinking of connectivity—to think so hard and fully of something else as to leave no room in the mind for the unwanted thought. He dwelt on the thought of Gala Tropile at enormous length and detail. He thought of the curve of her waist and her long, stringy hair, as well as her long, but not at all stringy, legs.

A lifetime's habits could not easily be overcome, and so from time to time an unbidden thought said, *Warning. Not your woman. Glenn Tropile's woman. Beware.* But, he reflected, where was Tropile, really? What possible harm could there be in thinking of his woman? Or, for that matter, of him?

It was really quite easy to think of that pretty and emotional woman, Gala Tropile, the Citizeness of Citizen Glenn Tropile, rather than connectivity. Citizen Germyn was pleased that he did it so well.

12

On Mount Everest, the sullen stream of off-and-on responses that was "mind" to the Pyramid had taken note of a new input signal from its ancillary systems on the home planet.

It was not a critical mind. Its only curiosity was a restless urge to shove-and-haul, and there was no shove-and-haul about what to it was perhaps the analogue of a man's hunger pang. The input signal said: Do thus.

It obeyed.

Call it craving for a new flavor. Where once it had patiently waited for the state that Citizens knew as meditation on connectivity, and the Pyramid itself perhaps knew as a stage of ripeness in the fruits of its wrist-watch mine, now it wanted a different taste. Unripe? Overripe? At any rate, different.

Accordingly, the h-f wheep, wheep changed in tempo and in key, and the bouncing echoes changed, and . . . and there was a ripe one to be plucked! (Its name was Innison.) And there another. (Gala Tropile.) And another, another— oh, a hundred others; a babe from Tropile's nursery school and the Wheeling jailer and a woman Tropile once had coveted on the street.

Once the ruddy starch-to-sugar mark of ripeness had been what human beings called Meditation on Connectivity and the Pyramids knew as a convenient blankness; now the sign was a sort of empathy with the Component named Tropile. Not just Tropile. The modulations of the input signal changed, and other signs of ripeness from other parts of the world were noted and acted upon, and so the Eyes swarmed over Cairo and Kiev and Khartoum. It didn't matter to the Pyramid. When a Component signaled readiness, it swung its electrostatic scythe; it harvested.

It did not occur to the Pyramid on Mount Everest that a Component might be directing its actions. How could it?

Perhaps the Pyramid on Mount Everest wondered, if it knew how to wonder, when it noticed that different criteria were involved in selecting Components these days. (If it knew how to "notice.") Surely even a Pyramid might wonder when, without warning or explanation, its orders were changed—not merely to harvest a different sort of Component, but to drag along with the flesh-and-blood needful parts a clanking assortment of machinery and metal, as began to happen. Machines? Why would the Pyramids need to Translate machines?

But why, on the other hand, would a Pyramid bother to question a directive, even if it were able to?

At any rate, it didn't. It swung its scythe, and gathered in what it was caused to gather in.

Men sometimes eat green fruit and come to regret it; it is the same with Pyramids.

And Citizen Germyn fell into the unsuspected trap. Avoiding connectivity, he thought of Glenn Tropile; and the unfelt h-f pulses found him out.

He didn't see the Eye that formed above him. He didn't feel the gathering of forces that formed his trap. He didn't know that he was: Seized, charged, catapulted through space, caught, halted and drained. It happened too fast.

One moment he was in his bed; the next moment he was—elsewhere. There wasn't anything between.

It had happened to hundreds of thousands of Components before him, but for Citizen Germyn what happened was in some ways different. He was not embalmed in nutrient fluid, formed and programmed to take his part in the Pyramid-structure; for he had not been selected by the Pyramid-structure but by the wild Component. He arrived conscious, awake, and able to move.

He stood up in a red-lit chamber. Vast crashes of metal buffeted his ears. Heat sprang little founts of perspiration on his skin.

It was too much, too much to take in at once. Oily-skinned madmen, naked, were capering and shouting at him. It took him a moment to realize that they were not devils; this was not Hell; he was not dead. "This way!" they were bawling at him. "Come on, hurry up!" He reeled, following their directions, across an unpleasantly warm floor, staggering and falling (the binary planet was a quarter lighter than Earth), until he got his balance.

The capering madmen led him through a door—or sphincter or trap; it was not like anything he had ever seen. But it was a portal of a sort, and on the other side of it was something closer to sanity. It was another room, and though the light was still red it was a paler, calmer red; and the thundering ironmongery was a wall away. The madmen were naked, yes; but they were not mad. The oil on their skins was only the sheen of sweat.

"Where—where am I?" he gasped.

Two voices, perhaps three or four, were all talking at once. He could make no sense of it. Citizen Germyn looked about him. He was in a sort of a chamber that formed a part of a machine that existed for the unknown purposes of the Pyramids on the binary planet. And he was alive—and not even alone.

He had crossed more than a million miles of space without feeling a thing. But when what the naked men were saying began to penetrate, the walls lurched around him. For a time the words were a meaningless noise. It wasn't the fall that hurt, it was the landing.

It was true; he had been Translated.

He looked dazedly down at his own bare body, and around at the room, and then he realized they were still talking: "—when you get your bearings. Feel all right now? Come on, Citizen, snap out of it!" Germyn blinked.

Another voice said peevishly: "There should be some other place to bring them in. That foundry isn't meant for human beings. Look at the shape this one is in! Some time somebody's going to come in, and we won't spot him in time, and—*pfut!*"

The first voice said: "Can't be helped. Hey! Are you all right?"

Citizen Germyn took a deep breath of the hot sour air and looked at the naked man before him. "Of course I'm all right," he said.

The naked man was Haendl.

There were several hundred of them. He learned that they were divided into eight natural groups. One group, Citizen Germyn's, was composed of people who had known Tropile. Another, given the clue of common-knowledge by Haendl, had conferred and decided that their link was acquaintance with one Citizeness Alla Narova, widow, of Nice. African origin and knowledge of one Django Tembo accounted for a third, and so on. They were spread through an acre of huge corridors primarily occupied by automatic machine tools which averaged eighty feet in height. Many were on legs, as though an ancient history of directly-operated machines irrationally dictated the shape of their fully-automatic descendants. Bars of metal sometimes abruptly popped into position as chuck jaws opened and then closed; then the metal bars began to spin, then tools advanced, sliced at them and retreated in order, and then the finished incomprehensible pieces would float away on just-visible annular magnetic fields. Every three hours a hexagonal forged plate floated in through the precisely-opened "door" of the foundry, clamped itself magnetically to one machine after another, and was drilled, bored, reamed, broached, milled, ground and polished into a greater mystery than it had been before. The toolbit, as tall as a man, of one slotting machine seemed to require regular replacement from a magazine after it worked on one of the hexagons, but the other tools did not noticeably lose their edges. Chips were carried away by a flood, every eleven hours or so, of glycerine. It came in jets from the walls, rose ankle-high, and gurgled down drainholes.

Once a Pyramid came by, gliding a handsbreadth off the floor and smelling of ozone. They hid like mice; they did not know whether the thing "saw" them or not.

They were fed from one set of taps in the wall and watered from another. Their water was a disgrace and an affront to the several Water Tasters among them, utterly lacking in the tang of carbonates and halogen salts. Their food was glucose syrup which must have been freighted with the necessary minerals and amino acids, for they did not fall sick of any deficiency disease. Their air was adequate—perhaps spillover from the adjoining foundry where an atmosphere was required for some of the processes.

Mostly, they waited and talked.

Citizen Germyn, for one, had a maggot in his brain about Translation. "Perhaps," he would say, "this really is Translation, really is bliss, and we lack only the wits to appreciate it. We have food, freedom from drastic temperature changes—" He slashed the sweat from his brow and went to the row of ever-running water faucets for a long drink before returning to his argument. "And there seems to be a sort of dispensation from ordinary manners and routine." He looked forlornly about him. No Husband's Chairs, no Wifely Chairs (decently armless). He squatted on the metal floor.

Haendl was more forthright. "Bliss, my foot! We're a bunch of damned Red Indians. I guess the Indians never knew what hit them. *They* didn't know about land grants and claiming territory for the crown, and about church missions and expanding populations. They didn't have those things. They learned by and by—at least about things like guns and firewater; they didn't have those things but they could see the sense to them. But I really don't think the Indians ever knew what the white men were up to until it was too late to matter. We're even deeper in the dark. At least the Indians had a clue now and then—they'd see the sailors come off the big white devil-ship and make a bee-line for their women; there was *something* in common. But we don't have that much. We're in the hands of the Pyramids—see? Our language! I have to say 'hands.' We don't even have a language to use about them!"

After about the fifieth time he had taken nourishment from the taps, Citizen Germyn ran tentatively amok. Luckily for all, it happened soon after one of the regular cleansings by glycerine; there were no sharp chips a foot long for him to use as daggers, and the floor was so slippery he couldn't keep his feet when he tried to strangle one of the Africans. People held his arms until he came to himself, bitterly chagrined.

"I am ready," he told them at last, with what dignity he could muster. "I realize that there is no proper catheter for a Donation, but withholding of air is an alternative method sanctified by tradition."

Innison told him not to be stupid, and added: "If you make a habit of amok we'll have to do something about you, but not until I figure a way to get you down an eight-inch drain."

It was a dreadful insult, delivered without so much as a Quirked Smile. Citizen Germyn could not bring himself to speak to Innison for three more feedings. Citizen Germyn's rage was such that he nerved himself up to turning his back on Innison in a marked manner; Innison was not only not crushed but did not even notice. He went right on talking to Haendl.

Citizen Germyn thereupon took Innison by

the hair with one hand and slapped him ringingly across the face with his other.

"Amok!" some of those nearby began to shout.

Haendl yelled back at them: "He is not! Shut up!" And to Germyn: "You aren't, are you?"

"No," Germyn snapped. "I'm just angry. Your disgusting friend here took it on himself to deny me the decent equivalent of a Donation which I deserve!"

Innison, rubbing his cheek, said thoughtfully: "You really want a Donation, boy? Where they stick the needle in and twist it around to find the canal? Then you go paralyzed, right then, and the fluid runs out. Then some simpering idiot takes the knife and saws it across your windpipe until it goes through—"

Germyn said: "Whether I *want* it or not is beside the point. There are certain decencies to be observed—"

"Then you *don't* want it?"

Germyn thought for a long while. "No," he finally said. "But that has nothing to do with . . ." He thought some more.

Haendl said gently: "Look at yourself, Germyn. Pinch yourself. Feel your arms and legs. You've changed. You grabbed Innison and you hit him, not in a nervous crisis but because you were angry. You wouldn't have done that not so long ago. Look at yourself."

Germyn looked. His stomach was flat; there was no trace at all of bloat. His thighs were now *thicker* than his knees—it had all happened so insidiously! He felt his face; under the beard it was fleshed, most Uncitizen-like, telling hardly at all of the skull beneath! His ribs—he couldn't see his ribs!

He faced them, burning with shame for his grotesqueness and saw they were the same, they were all the same.

"And don't you *feel* different?" Haendl insisted quietly. "Inside, all through you? Didn't you used to have an all-through-you feeling that would have kept you from hitting Innison? Don't you now have an all-through-you feeling that tells you hitting Innison, within reason, would be a joy?"

"I do," said Germyn in terror. "I do! What do you call it? What shall I do about it?"

"It's orthodox Wolf opinion," Innison said, "that you shouldn't do anything about that feeling. And the accepted name for it is, not being hungry. Have you been meditating on connectivity lately?"

"No," said Germyn. "The—the distractions—"

"The absence of hunger, Germyn. Starvation and meditation go together, though not inseparably. When your vitality's low, your self-awareness flickers; it's always ready to be blown out."

Germyn wandered off through a forest of machine-tool legs, trying to get acquainted with his new self.

Haendl said to Innison: "Maybe that's why we're here, to get nice and plump."

"You think they eat people?"

"No; not any more than a fusion pile does. It's got to be something electrical . . ."

"If *Germyn's* ready and able to fight, all of 'em ought to be. Suppose we get a little close-order drilling organized."

"We'd better get something organized. There haven't been any more amoks, but there's been a lot of pushing-around. Next you get counter-pushing, and then people start swinging."

The two Wolves grinned at each other. "It lasted just fine, didn't it?" Haendl said. "Cul-chah and aesthetics petered out the first week on unlimited calories, and then went manners—usually with a crash, like ex-Citizen Germyn. Yes, we've got to give them something to do before they get *fat* and begin killing one another."

New people stopped arriving in the foundry about then; when twelve feeding-times passed with no recruits turning up the Princeton Wolves took a census: six hundred and eighty-four, roughly half male and half female. This was a great convenience, for one could not talk forever.

The military organization got under way with some difficulty. The ex-Citizens were glorying in new-found truculence. "Who's gonna make me?" rang joyously through the corridors; a research-minded Princetonian recalled that some Biblical person had "waxed fat and wicked." A combination of force and reason carried the day, however, and at last the most obstreperous ex-Citizen, his black eye fading slowly, marched in ranks with the rest. Haendl yearned for the weapons that had been Translated; where were they?

And then several women were in early pregnancy. The pregnancies all occurred following an incident as inexplicable as it was horrifying. A Pyramid came again, and again they hid. This time luck had it that one of the Africans was caught in the open, some distance from a wall and a hopeless long dash to the tangle of I-beams which supported the giant tools. He did the prudent thing and flattened himself against the floor, probably feeling reasonably safe in his last seconds of life. The giant figure sailed slowly down the corridor with plenty of clearance on either side, crackling faintly, smelling of ozone. Approaching the huddled man, it swerved calmly so that its nearest corner brushed over him, and then moved on and out of the corridor through one of the un-doorlike doors of Pyramid engineering.

They had no difficulty at all putting the African down an eight-inch drain, and the sleeping-time that followed was marked by an orgy. The men did not practice the Loving Withdrawal, nor would the women have let them. Doom was on them, and instinct in command.

Wolves and Sheep, or ex-Sheep, endlessly debated the crushing of the African.

"We're here because they brought us here. They must want us for something. Why did they destroy something they carefully imported and kept alive and more or less comfortable?"

"Maybe the sight of us annoys them. Maybe

we're stockpiled but they just don't want us pestering them until they're ready for us."

"Maybe it did it for fun."

"I don't believe it. Your white man didn't do it to those Indians of yours."

"Some of them did. Some of them shot Indians for fun. Maybe there are some Pyramids that are different from other Pyramids. Maybe that one was a cruel child!"

They threw up their hands and left it at that.

What else was there to do? None among them knew any more than any other what the Pyramids wanted, thought or were likely to do.

What else there was to do was to stand ever ready to dash for shelter; to post guards with relay-runners at both of the "doors" and the entrance to the foundry. They did this, for what it might be worth.

But no Pyramids came after that.

And one day in the second month of the pregnancies the woman Gala Tropile was talking to suddenly screamed. She pointed to the wall in terror. Gala turned, and then she screamed, too.

Something was gnawing a hole in the wall.

The crowd that gathered jittered to each other in fear, but whatever was chewing a hole in the wall did not seem to be a Pyramid. It didn't seem to be anything that made sense at all.

The crowd watched as a circular area of

metal, something over a meter across, was outlined by a flying dot that bulged the ductile stuff up into a ridge. The flying dot holed through. It was a toolbit. The cut-out disk clanged on the floor.

The nearest in the crowd screamed and jumped back.

Then the toolbit and its spinning holder withdrew. There was a long pause. One of the sweaty, scared men—it was a Russian from Kiev—dared to try to peer into the hole, but there was nothing to see, only blackness and the distant, retreating drill.

Minutes later a black cone stuck its point out of the hole and spoke to them:

"Pay close attention. To speak to you in this way is very difficult. You have been brought here for a purpose. Henceforth you will receive orders from this communications system. Follow the orders at once, completely. Are the food and water sufficient?"

The voice made Gala Tropile shiver, for it was nothing like human. (But what was that curiously familiar hint of tone?) However, since it asked questions, presumably it wanted answers. She ventured one: "There is enough, but it's terribly monotonous. Couldn't we have different flavors now and then?"

"No. You do not understand. Feeding you is very difficult. Also it is an advantage that you are bored. Is your chief person listening?"

Haendl and Innison began to speak at once; there was a fierce, brief duel of eyes which Innison lost. "I'm listening," Haendl said.

"These are the rules of communication with us. You notice a humming from this loudspeaker. We now cause the humming to stop." The faint hum stopped and started again. "When the loudspeaker is humming you may consider it 'on' and speak into it. When the loudspeaker is not humming you will consider it 'off.' Since this is merely a psychological trick and the loudspeaker is never really off, you will see to it by posting guards that we are not addressed except when we want to be addressed."

"I understand," said Haendl, wishing he dared to add some ironical honorific. He was frightened. The voice was non-human; it had never come from a warm, moist pair of lungs, swept over vibrating cartilage, resonated in the sculptured caverns of the head and emerged shaped by muscular lips and tongue. The voice was a modulated electronic output, a skillful blend of a dozen vibrating crystals. It was as cold as crystal. This he had dared to dream of attacking! With small arms and a tank and a helicopter!

The loudspeaker still buzzed faintly. Fear and all, it was an opportunity to talk with a Pyramid, to ask it what was in store for them, for all of humanity. As far as he knew, nobody had ever done so. He drew his breath ready to make some history, but a woman, the widow of the slain African, pushed him aside and yelled into the black cone: "Why did you kill my husband? What did he do to you that you crushed him flat?"

"We did not kill your husband," said the black cone. "That was done by a Pyramid."

"Who are you then, damn you?" Haendl shouted.

"We are best known to you as Glenn Tropile," said the loudspeaker, and then the hum stopped; no amount of pleading or cursing would get it started again.

13

No Sicilian or Pole on Ellis Island, no American tourist caught in the bureaucracy of a French hotel had ever been as much of a stranger in town as Glenn Tropile. He knew *nothing*. To put it more precisely, he knew everything several decades of life had taught him, as Citizen and as Wolf.

But no part of that knowledge was in any way relevant to his present existence as one-eighth of the Snowflake.

Tropile, however, was Wolf. He was nearly Pyramid, in that he pushed until something gave, and dissected until he found bits that could be managed.

For example, there was a more or less manageable bit close at hand. The communications systems that joined one petal of the Snowflake to the others were relatively easy to penetrate, and that was quickly done.

Tropile and Alla Narova had awakened the

woman between them, apprehensive of further hysterics. There were none. She was Mercedes van Dellen of Istanbul, 28 clock-years old at the time of her Translation, and a mother of two girls who had been small when she left them. She sighed and supposed they were happily married by now. She was interested and amused by the input-display and her busily-clicking hands; she confided that she liked to keep busy and (mild blasphemy) she would have had a dozen babies if it had been permitted. They felt into her mind; it was calm, always calm. So there really *were* people like that! She felt into theirs. They were fierce and impassioned; my goodness, don't they get all worked up about nothing! And then the three of them flowed together; this time it was more limpid and even.

They awakened a brown-skinned woman who also appeared to be in her late twenties, but her body was a lie. The soul of Kim Seong was the soul of a bitter hag who had seen all come and seen all go, who washed corpses for her rice and mumbled: "It's foolishness, it's all foolishness, but what's the good of talking? Nobody listens to you."

She added to the pool of mind a bitterness and their first hint of comprehending the infinite reaches of space and the two eternities before and behind, too vast for meaning.

They awakened Corso Navarone of Milan, a thin young man who knew just what it was all about. He was in Love with Alla Narova as he had never Loved before. All space and time had conspired to bring them together; he was her soul, she was his flame; never had there been such a Love as theirs. What matter that an accident of surgery prevented the consummation of desire? They were together; it was enough. Hold off, ye gods, further bliss, lest Corso Navarone perish of delight.

They couldn't believe he was real, but they had to; there he was. He refused indignantly at first to surrender his individuality to the pool, but was argued into it; how better could he know his beloved? And, once in, he wanted to stay forever and had to be argued out of it; did not absence make the heart grow fonder?

To their shared consciousness he brought fire.

The old man they awakened was one Spyros Gulbenkian. Tropile felt himself abashed before him to have claimed the name of Wolf. Spyros was a wolfpack all by himself, in a quiet way. Half Paris had worked for him and never known it for a second. His life had been incredibly busy; incidents crowded it like watchworks, and from each passing minute he had learned a new thing, a new tool or weapon, and he never forgot. He was mightily amused; he woke without shock or fear. "So I've cheated death!" he said, delighted. "The one thing I never hoped for! Now what is this Group Mind you tell me about? There's no question of my being stubborn, of course—I owe you people a great deal!"

Tropile: "It's power—sheer power. You think

faster, clearer and more deeply than you ever believed possible."

Alla Narova: "It's being more intensely yourself. It's feeling utterly alive."

Mercedes van Dellen: "It's very pleasant. I'm not sure what we *do* when we're that way, but it's nothing wrong."

Kim Seong: "It's no more foolish than anything else."

Corso Navarone: "Foolish woman, it is bliss!"

Spyros Gulbenkian: "Hmmm." But try it he did, and they found him welcome as ballast; he kept them from making mistakes. Before him in a brief session they had calculated the number of molecules in the universe; with him they did it again—this time, right.

All he wanted to know was: "Where did the mathematics come from? I'm aware that none of us is a mathematician, and I don't trust something-for-nothing, ever!"

"I think the mathematics came out of the world," Tropile said. "I think mathematics is just a picture of the world. If you have eyes and ears and enough brain, you have mathematics. We had enough brain. I notice that we don't have botany, except for Kim's Lichen Shades Cult."

"As long as it is not something for nothing," Spyros Gulbenkian said. "Shall we have some words with the large black gentleman who is sleeping with his mouth open? What splendid teeth! Teeth alone are all I mourn from my youth."

So they greeted the seventh petal, Django

Tembo of Africa. He woke to them yawning and smiling, good-humored. He alone of them had dreamed, long and pleasant dreams of wives and children. He had been an Untouchable dung-carrier in Durban, but somehow his heart was the heart of a king. He lived to serve by commanding, and by commanding to serve. They read his noble, guileless soul and fell in love with it, and he with theirs.

The last branch of the snowflake was unprepossessing. It was the body of a scrawny youth with an ill-shaped head and coarse black hair. They felt their way into his consciousness and memory, and found not much of either. *Me Willy*. Shifting planes of color, somehow sad—they knew it was sunset beyond the crags of Sonora, but he did not. *Mama go. Mama pretty*. A brown bulk with people in it; it made him dully wonder why, but they knew the Las Cruces House of Five Regulations, and how within a year he would have Donated under Regulation Two (anent Innocents). *Beans good. Beans with honey good*.

They conferred in dismay on what they had found. "We'd be crippling ourselves!" Tropile cried.

"I don't know about that," said Mercedes van Dellen unexpectedly. "The poor child never had a chance. His mother must have left him. Did you ever hear such longing and unhappiness?"

Tropile, like all Lucifers, Captain Flandrays, Byrons, Duquesnes and other sardonic folk, was convinced that there was no sorrow like unto his sorrow; he thought surely that Mercedes van Dellen might have known as much. He fell sulkily silent.

Kim Seong cackled that it was all one to her; the difference between an idiot and the wisest man who ever was did not make any difference to anything as far as she could see. She enjoyed their consternation.

Django Tembo decided for them. They invited Willy to join them not with words and syllogisms but by opening like a flower and letting him be the butterfly. His shy animal soul flowed into theirs and they were richer by it. He had been an animal, with an animal's powers of joy and sorrow, undiluted by apprehension for the one or philosophical consolations for the other.

Spyros Gulbenkian later said wistfully: "Perhaps being young was not so bad after all." This was during a brief spell during which they disengaged and were themselves apart again. Such spells became briefer and more infrequent.

Chiefly the Snowflake floated in its tank and thought in its own mode, in eight-part counterpoint rather than in human melodic lines. Sometimes it thought in chord progressions, battering at problems and questions until they yielded.

Ceaselessly it did its work for the Pyramids; no second went past without the sixteen hands' clicking manipulation of their switches. Ceaselessly it did its own work of analysis and planning. The difference was that for the Pyramids it did its work with eight times Rashevsky's number of switchings; for itself it worked with Rashevsky's Number of switchings to the eighth power.

In human transcript, the Snowflake began by exhausting all its memories and arranging them for ready access—the ancient dream accomplished at last. Did an off-color rice grain in three-year-old Kim Seong's Korean bowl fit into a problem? It was there. Must Corso Navarone remember *the* serial number of a bicycle that whizzed past him in Milan *one* Friday when he was twelve? He remembered. If a persuasive shrug of Spyros Gulbenkian thirty years ago in Paris was of use, they had it when it was needed.

The Snowflake decided: "I am unfulfilled. Sex does not matter, for immortality is possible to me. Love does not matter, for I have more than love. What matters is increasing my store of sense-data, and taking readings off scales."

But when this was done the Snowflake was not satisfied. There was something about the sum of its individual memories taken as a whole that totaled more than the sum of each individual one of them. There was a collective memory of some kind.

For some reason, it seemed rather urgent.

So the Snowflake put its collective mind to work, and after a time was able to remember what that collective memory was about.

Oh, yes, humanity.

The human race was in trouble.

At first the Snowflake (trying one thing, then another) thought that bringing human beings to the binary planet would, at least, rescue those particular individuals from their trouble. The Snowflake did that for a while, since it was so easy, relatively speaking, to redefine "ripeness" for the Pyramid on Mount Everest. (The Mount Everest Pyramid, of course, did not question its directives. The Pyramids collected ripe Components when available, according to the ancient maxim of "Take a chicken when you can." It never occurred to any Pyramid that their Components might stockpile Components.)

Then the Snowflake discovered there were other possibilities.

Among the million million systems that filled the binary planet were a great number whose functions were construction, maintenance and repair. All of these were semi-intelligent and semi-autonomous, which is to say they were directed by controlling mechanisms—by other Components.

What would happen, the Snowflake wondered, if they were to try to awaken some of these others?

When they tried it, it was very nearly a disaster. They chose to begin with a tunnel-digging system that had not been used for some forty thousand years. Its Components were not at all human. What made it really bad was that they were soft-bodied slugs no longer than a thumb; on their home world they had clung to the underside of great jungle leaves, and their worst enemy was a primate-looking sort of arboreal mollusc which hunted them out and ate them. When they realized what sort of creature's mind was touching theirs they went mad with fear. The drilling machine corkscrewed and curlicued shafts through a dozen major power centers. Battalions of repair systems raced into action to deal with the damage. It was a very high probability that a Pyramid itself might before long come sailing by, to see what was wrong.

Fortunately, Tropile's Snowflake still had firm control over Component selection and replacement. The Snowflake sadly dumped the mad Components into the recycling hoppers, and took thought for the future.

It was not a good idea to awaken Components at random.

Therefore it would be best merely to issue commands.

There was a way of doing that without detection. It relied on the redundancy of Pyramid-system commands. As a fail-safe measure, every click of their controls was repeated.

Thereafter the Snowflake began to malfunction, as far as the Pyramids were concerned, on a level below detectability. Man's idiot servant the thermostat is not, except in laboratories, set to perform with knife-edge precision; there is always some tolerance. In an automobile of the Car Age the radiator thermostat was doing well if it opened and closed within a range of ten degrees. Home oil-burner thermostats were more precise, operating to plus or minus a degree, but what is a degree? It is ten thousand ten-thousandths of a degree, a million millionths of a degree. There is always room for improvement, so much room that no engineer bothers beyond the area significant to him.

The Snowflake was allowed one false transmission per thousand-odd clicks; the process in which it was engaged would not suffer from such a tolerance. There is no perfection. There is no sense in doing the work that insures one thousand clicks out of one thousand are dead-sure accurate—except when your thermostat is part Wolf.

In the Pyramid's work upon which the Snowflake was engaged, it was now assigned to send messages to automatic machinery throughout the binary planet; it was building propulsion units from scratch, procurement, logistics and all. It started by scouring the planet for surplus material; it was continuously scrounging. A zinc torus in live storage would be scrutinized; it would be determined that it was last used during the Magellanic Raid as a weapons component, that in this section of the Galaxy there were no life-forms susceptible to that type of weapon (it produced a sort of marbled fog whose sight was death to the Color Sculptors of the Magellanic Cloud). The torus floated then, at the right time, to the right place to be alloyed into material for the emitter of an ion gun which would be sub-assembled later, and still later go into the master assembly, and still later take its proper place for maximum push when the binary next corrected its course towards more Components.

One click per thousand was false. This was low tolerance, and sensibly set that way: the Snowflake's job was of such versatility that errors could not possibly be cumulative. It switched from this task to that continuously. Had the false clicks been random, they would have caused the zinc torus to wobble on its way to smelting, or recognizably wrong information about its function to have been applicable to dielectrics instead of conductors, say, which would have given the Snowflake pause and made it ask again.

The false clicks accumulated surprisingly. Sixteen hands delivered eighty clicks per second; by Earth-clock almost 700 thousand per day. So, five hundred times a day—margin for safety!—a cunningly-vectored error went out. The zinc toruses did not wobble except sometimes, and wrong information came in but seldom. Instead, machine-tools moved jerkily, like time-lapse photography of an opening flower. Bit by bit a queer electron tube was formed in a deserted shop. A reserve of errors was accumulated for five days and a bar was swiftly zone-refined in another; zone-melting cannot be done in time-lapse. From this were sawed and assembled transistors. In a month's time the Snowflake, slave of the Pyramids, had a slave of its own, a Black Box of its own, programmed to drive a hair-fine copper wire from itself to the Snowflake's tank, and this it did at a mile an hour for fifty hours.

When it arrived, the Revolt of the Thermostat had fairly begun. The Petal needed no longer to hoard its allowance of false pulses or calculate a thousand alternatives before determining which click would be most economical and strategic. The hair-fine wire homed on the switch in the left hand of Alla Narova's petal. At the moment it made contact, the Snowflake convulsed and shifted the burden of output from her left hand to the fifteen hands remaining. Communication was now direct. "Errors" might move raw material to the idiot-box at the end of the wire which knew only how to make and move wire at present. Over that wire it would learn how to shape the raw materials into glass eyes and metal arms and rolling high-polymer feet.

It was tucked away in a corridor adjoining a foundry. The Snowflake ordered it to scan the corridor and report. The Snowflake decided: "That corridor will do for our mice." It commissioned the slave, growing every day in size and complexity, to tap the binary's water system and install a row of faucets along the corridor wall, and then to make up a decent nutrient mix by stealing glucose and whatever minerals and amino acids were required from the millenially-ancient tangle of piping that overlayed and undermined the metabolic-products area of the planet, and to conduct the mix via another row of faucets to the same corridor.

The Snowflake decided: "We will now explore the planet."

Not experimentally but by design they programmed their slavish Black Box, every hour less the idiot, to send out spies. They went forth like small spiders, their metallic shine dulled by lampblack. Their eightfold eyes scanned corridors, tubes, wires, vats, reactors. Machines were built to build machines to build spies; spy-types modified rapidly by descent. There were long-range primary scouts, tarantula-like because they needed fair-sized power packs for speed and range, small-headed because they scanned only in a general way. A week later there were more thoughtful, analytic types, carried pick-a-back by tarantulas in pairs. These had egg-heads, crammed with eyes, ears, noses, thermocouples, ion counters, spectrophotometers. For coarse measurement of space some went out in tandem, each the eye of a rangefinder of variable base-line. For fine measurement there were the tiny ones who clicked off exactly a millimeter at each step and who had antennae exactly one micron in diameter.

The Snowflake learned how many Pyramids there were on the binary: seven.

The spies watched them continuously and the Snowflake learned to know one Pyramid from another. They were only approximately the same size; there was a largest and a smallest. There were appreciable differences of strength, pattern and rate of change in the electromagnetic fields that surrounded each of them. One of them was a glutton. It repaired much more often than the others to the metabolic-products complex, but it was a difference of degree and not of an order of magnitude. They all consumed many tons of chemicals each clockday, absorbing them from a pelting spray that surrounded them on their three non-propulsive sides.

So much the Snowflake learned about the Pyramids. After months of intensive study they had the answers to a thousand questions about them . . . though not, of course, to the questions that really mattered. Like:

Why did the Pyramids do what they did? And,

Where did they come from? And, most of all,

How could they be defeated?

It was always a great temptation to the Snowflake to try to awaken other human Components. They debated the question often among themselves. "We could use some help," Alla Narova would say, and Spyros Gulbenkian would snap, "They would betray us to the Pyramids!" and Tropile would snarl, "We've already made our decision on this. Let's stick to it!" And then on another day perhaps Glenn Tropile, dismayed by the immensity of their task and the slow rate at which it was going, might venture, "Well, maybe we could just trying awakening *one* other human." And Alla Narova would flash, "No! Oh, no! You were

right, it's too dangerous," and Willy would
gently say, "Please. Please. Don't fight, please."

The non-human Components were less of a
temptation, because that first terrifying experience had not been forgotten. All the same,
they were interesting. There were so many of
them! There were soft-bodied creatures and
chitinous ones, things with legs, or fins, or
feathers—one bunch had all three. The pre-
ponderant chemistry was C_2 and H_2O, like
Earth's, but there were also methane-breathers,
and silicon-based organisms . . . well, no, "organisms" might be the wrong word, because
the tiny, faceted, filamenterous beings made
of tainted silicon ate not, neither did they
breathe; light turned itself into electricity on
their body surfaces; they seemed to grow by
accreting silicon dust on their external areas,
and reproduce by splitting along defined lines
of cleavage.

How many separate races were involved?

Even with all its other preoccupations, the
Snowflake's curiosity drove it to try to estimate the number. It was impossible to be
precise, because the discovery that the pur-
plish banana-shaped wrigglers and the mos-
quitoid creatures the size of a roc were simply
sexually dimorphic versions of the same being
cast doubt on all calculations. Especially since
a number of other species seemed to alter
forms as they grew. Nevertheless the Snowflake achieved an estimate:

Not less that 480, nor probably more than

600, different species had been kidnapped as Components for the Pyramids.

The next calculation that occurred to the curiosity of the Snowflake was far easier to make, but far more disturbing.

From the Pyramids' navigation systems they learned that the next planetfall was still over a thousand years away. Nor was that a particularly long voyage for the Pyramid planet. Under average, if anything.

So . . .

Assuming that an average trip lasted two thousand years. Assuming that at least half of the target planets did, in fact, fail to produce Components worth harvesting. Assuming that the Components already observed represented separate planets of origin. . . .

Then the Snowflake's best guess was that the Pyramids had been busy wandering around the Galaxy and doing their thing for something like—

Two

Million

Years.

When the Snowflake attained that estimate they contemplated it in stark silence for a moment.

Then they began to laugh. What else was there to do?

Some of the races who did the Pyramids' work were pretty thin on the ground—a dozen of this, only a handful of that. No doubt they were the oldest. No doubt most of the earliest

Components had finally worn out, as living things ultimately must. First In, First Out. When their error factors began to exceed permitted levels they would have been honorably retired from service. (That is, recycled to make soups for the survivors.)

One creature in particular seemed special. It was not exactly a Component, it seemed. What it exactly *was* became a source of considerable argument among the members of the Snowflake.

It was in a special place, to begin with: the North Pole. And it seemed to be the principal subject of in-person attention from the Pyramids. It was a creature with an elephantine, blue-green body with a chitinous armor and seven tentacles. This creature lay in state under a crystal dome at the North pole of the binary, in the largest compartment the planet could boast beneath its skin—the only one of a size to accommodate all seven Pyramids and presumably the eighth from Everest. The other peculiarity of this huge room and its surrounding complex was that no Components, human or non-human, none of the living Black Boxes, were wired into the circuits serving it. Instead, crude-looking hydraulic actuators opened valves and closed switches under the direct pressure of electron beams sprayed from the Pyramids' apexes. The seven monsters puttered endlessly with the different eighth monster. They flooded its chamber of crystal with benign fluids in various proportions, with gases at different partial pressures. They set up worn old electrostatic generators and got them moving so that weak charges might be built up under the crystal dome. (Certainly, since they could themselves produce electrical charges directly, the generators must have been "tweezers").

And nothing ever came of it. By and by it became clear that the experiments were being repeated. Perhaps the word was Ritual.

The Snowflake pondered over this for a long time. Finally Spyros Gulbenkian, the oldest of the eight, whose memories went back before the Pyramids came crashing and grabbing into the world of men, said doubtfully, "I saw a tellyfilm once. It was an old movie, American, but I think about a place in Germany, where a mad scientist tries to bring back to life a dead man. Its name was *Frankenstein*."

Alla Narova laughed. "I know that story," she said. "It can have nothing to do with us."

"And why is that?" demanded Gulbenkian.

"Because Dr. Frankenstein was only trying to create a monster," she explained. "Why would the Pyramids need to create a monster? When they already have us?"

But intellectual curiosity did not fully occupy the Snowflake. Under Glenn Tropile's urging they kept industriously at the principal occupation of any Wolf, namely to keep on trying things until something worked.

They had long since succeeded in corrupting the Everest Pyramid. The Components programmed to Plug-in-or-Stockpile newly-arrived Components had been reached. Thereafter the

Everest Pyramid was bedevilled by the fact
that *all* its shipped Components were stockpiled. There was need, crying need for new
Components, but the ones it sent went into
Stockpile! It stepped up its shipments, and at
last by chance scythed down and fired off to
the binary planet one of Tropile's acquaint-
ances and one of Django Tembo's. These were
not stockpiled; the next fifty arrivals were.
Ahah! The pattern became clear on Everest.
One shipped from Princeton and from Durban
and possibly other places . . . yes, *six* other
places, it appeared at length.

Once it had learned, there came to the Snowflake the job of deactivating existing components in circuit, faking a demand. At last six
hundred and eighty-four folk known to branches
of the Snowflake were on hand, and the Snowflake holed a transceiver through their corridor wall and told them: "Henceforth your
directions will come from us . . ."

14

For a little while Gala Tropile was almost a
queen of the mad and ragged little band. She
had status enough for that as the wife (or was
it the widow?) of the voice from the black
cone. Having benefited from Tropile's tutor-
ing during their abrasive marriage, she was
Wolf enough to take advantage of that fact.
For nearly two days Gala Tropile waved others imperiously out of the way at the feeding
pipes and chose the best places to sleep. Only
for two days. The reason her reign didn't last
longer was that she was by no means the only
Wolf around.

Besides, the voice from the black cone wasn't
always Tropile's.

It was all very confusing.

Directions came now and then from the
loudspeaker cone to the people in the corridor. Metallic spiders came and eyed them,
and went away again. The people tried to

question the voices from the loudspeaker, and
they always got answers, but seldom the answers they wanted to hear. Or that even made
sense:

"What do you want with us, damn you?"

"We want you to be mice," said the black
cone.

Mice? How mice? Why mice? But the cone
had fallen into one of its silences again.

Then:

"Sometimes you say you're Tropile, sometimes you say you're this Django Tembo or
somebody else. Who are you?"

"Yes."

It was absolutely infuriating. Ragged-nerved,
the corridor people squabbled among themselves. They did not dare outright violence, at
least at first; it was not a good idea to end an
argument by punching your opponent out,
when you were starkly aware that next time
you slept he might stay awake, waiting. So
they took out their fury on their surroundings,
smashing, damaging, ruining. (Very like mice.)
And still tried to get sensible answers:

"What—exactly, please!—are you going to
do with us?"

"We will tell you," said the voice—Tropile's
this time, as it happened. And it added, "Soon
we will begin to starve you."

"*Starve? Why? When? What for?*"

"To make you mousier. Soon."

And when they could get no further answers from the black cone, the marooned band
tried to prepare for this new, intolerable ag-

gravation. They would have stored up food and water if they could. They couldn't. Their raw materials were only the chips from the giant machine tools, and they were good tools; they made minimum chips. The lathes pared off helices of metal and plastic which were pretty and next to useless. The milling machines shaved off long needles that fell in showers to be washed away by the periodic inundation of the shop. They tried bending the helices back and forth to snap off slightly-distorted squares of metal from them, and they did. They bundled the milling machine chips to make stakes and hammers, and tried to pound their metal squares into storage pots, and it just didn't work. If the metal that peeled from the lathes happened to be brittle enough to snap into plates, it could not be ductile enough to draw into pots. Three attempts to anneal the plates in the adjoining foundry's terrible heat ended fatally; the place was impossibly dangerous. One grew faint and vague in the heat and bad air; one stumbled—into a naked high-tension cable, or a bubbling crucible, or onto the die of a champing automatic hammer. They were apprehensive, and bored, and nasty-tempered and well-fed—just what the Snowflake wanted them to be.

In its almost-final stage of evolution, the Snowflake could hardly have been seen in its tank by an outside observer, there were so many wires. It had long ago delegated its Pyramid-assigned task to an octet in a spare tank; there had been no difficulty in duplicat-

ing the input-board or the output-switches,
but the programming of the octet at double-
remote control had been insanely difficult, demanding total recall of the Snowflake's own
programming and its duplication, step by step,
upon the spare. Once this had been done,
however, and all sixteen hands were freed,
the Snowflake had the freedom of the binary.
Its wires and cables went everywhere; gradually its metal spider-spies were retired, for
the Snowflake acquired direct-reporting eyes
and transducers of its own. It diverted and
armor-plated a supply of its nutrient fluid calculated to last out any emergency; it co-opted
generators to stand by ready to be cut in upon
any power failure of its pumps; it shielded
itself in steel, soft iron, lead and cadmium
against physical, magnetic and radiational attack; it mounted itself and its whole huge
supply-complex in caterpillar treads.

The spider-spies continued to serve it only
in one area: the chamber under the North
Pole. It was felt that the deliberate archaism
of the great room's equipment argued against
insinuating its scanners there. If a cable crawled
down a conduit of the nutrients area it was of
no concern to a Pyramid going by. That was
what Componets were for—to lay cables in
the right places at the right time. Under general directives they did so. No quantity of
transducers turning up throughout the binary
could be a cause for alarm; doubtless it was
some quality- or traffic-control system going
into effect to ensure the continuance of the

Pyramid's environment without cost or care to them while they—did what?

While they performed their interminable round of experiments on the tentacled creature under the crystal dome. Performed them in slow and stately tempo, slower than their normal motions down corridors, or their flares of electrons to manipulate relays, damping rods or pinch fields.

"I wish—" said Glenn Tropile fretfully. He didn't have to finish the sentence. Alla Narova finished it for him.

"I, too, wish we knew what that was all about," she said, "but we don't."

When the Snowflake tired of wondering about the North Pole, it could get a little variety in its collective life by wondering about the South.

The most interesting thing about the South Pole was that it was so uninteresting. Nothing ever went there, neither Pyramid nor Component-driven mechanism. Nothing seemed to take place inside it. There were no Eyes there, no instruments to detect. The best guess of the Snowflake (actually, the only one it had) was that it was a junk heap.

"Archeologists," declared Corso Navarone, "find all sorts of interesting things in junk heaps. Let us look at this one."

So, from its locus at South Latitude 12, the Snowflake began to manufacture and drive southward a special cable, coaxial and filled with inert gas, a marvelous nerve trunk over which the most complex messages could be sent and received. The intuition was that this would be the case. Through the lowest levels of the undermined planet crawled a caterpillar-tread device, heaving the cable behind it. It extended a teflon snout into chambers of corrosive atmosphere and skirted them; it shunned the red-lit storage and access spaces for the lower, darker tubes bored through bedrock, not yet crammed with pipes and wires, not yet visited incessantly by scuttling repair-machines. Its outriders, tapped into the cable, rolled inertly along, waiting with machine patience for their tasks. One squad of them was an excavation group—derricks, angledozers, mining machines that undercut, blasted and wiped up debris with scything paws onto an endless belt that shunted it away from the field of operation. Another group, echeloned behind the excavators, consisted of transducers— artificial sense organs of every kind, very cold and scientific, reporting themselves coldly in scribed curves, needles jogging on scales, counter-readings, whining modulations of whining carrier waves. And behind them, almost apologetically, rolled self-propelled color-image orthicon tubes, mere television, which reported only pictures, surfaces—not even X-ray deep.

The voice of ex-Citizen Roget Germyn was ragged with nerves. He snarled at Muhandas Dutta of Durban: "Get away from the tap. You saw me headed for it. Then you got up and started to it."

Muhandas Dutta, formerly a leading exponent of the Rice Tasting Cult, well on his way toward a Grand Mastership in it, snarled back: "I've better things to do with my time than notice who's wandering across the floor. I was here first, flat-belly."

The epithet was foolish; the belly of Muhandas Dutta was quite as free from honorable hunger-bloat as that of Roget Germyn. But old things mixed with the new. "Muscle boy!" Germyn sneered. "Gobbler! Shouter! Strider!" Schoolyard epithets, and he was shouting them. The tap bubbled quietly between them as they stood with veins distended, fists clenched and eyes bulging; its sticky glucose solution bore the precious iron, iodine, sulfur, phosphorus, potassium along in an unending runnel down the slightly-slanting floor to the eight-inch drain. Glutamic acid, without which ammonia accumulates in the brain and kills, dribbled along the floor while they glared, and D-ribose, and D-2-deoxyribose, adenine, guanine, uracil, cytosine, thymine and 5-methyl cytosine without which no thing higher than a trilobite can pass on its shape and meaning to its next generation. Over the rivulet of life they glared, ignoring the long row of bubbling taps they might have resorted to at their right and their left; this one is mine, mine! Be damned to sense, be damned to abundance; kindness be damned to hell; it's mine!

A Wolf, now red-eyed not with feral lust

but with fatigue from his endless job of keeping the peace, ambled over. "Break it up," said Haendl. Muhandas Dutta was nervously clutching the dagger-like milling machine chip thrust through his loin cloth, all that remained of a Citizen's decent robes. Haendl turned his back on him and the dagger, stooped and took a long swig at the bubbling tap. There was some stir of action behind him; at his leisure he straightened up and turned around. Dutta had drawn his weapon and aimed it; before the plunge Germyn had seized his wrist. They stood now locked and straining silently. Haendl wrenched the dragger from Dutta's weakening grasp and tossed it along the floor, clattering. The strained tableau collapsed; the men panted and glared, Dutta rubbing his wrist.

"Everybody's nerves are on edge," Haendl lectured them. "The fact that everybody's nerves are apparently *supposed* to be on edge doesn't matter. We've got to be a little more gracious, or we'll all wind up in a mutual massacre. Dutta and Germyn, suppose you pretend that I'm very old and wise and take my advice. There's a perfectly good food tap over there for you, Dutta, and a perfectly good one for you, Germyn, as soon as that Russian fellow's through with it. I suggest each of you go to his own tap and fill up."

"Flatbelly!" Dutta sneered, but he went, looking over his shoulder at Germyn.

"Muscle boy!" Germyn sneered, and he went to his tap, not turning his back on the African.

Then they bent to drink, but then there was nothing to drink.

With a final bubble the taps ceased to run, and did not start again.

Pandemonium spread through the acre of corridors. People came stumbling and sobbing to the taps. The door guards and the relay of runners deserted their posts and raced to the food taps. Some licked at the floor where the last of the sticky stuff was drying, awaiting the glycerine inundation. A few lucky ones battered their way to the eight-inch drains and thrust their arms down them as far as they could go, smearing and coating their arms and hands with what clung to the sides of the drainpipes; then they licked at themselves like cats.

Haendl, who had only a few minutes ago been savagely amused that his role was to keep ex-Citizens from tearing one another apart, to urge them towards graciousness and consideration, was now not amused. He said to Innison, the two apart from the churning mob: "Next the water goes off. Next, of course, we start spreading out and, I suppose, dying—most of us." They walked to the black cone of the loudspeaker-microphone; the guards who should be there to shield whatever was at the other end from vain importunings were away. The black cone was humming, which meant that it might be addressed. But Haendl backed away, drew Innison with him and said: "I'm damned if I will. I'm damned if I'll give it a chance to tell us to be good mice."

*   *   *

The phalanx of machinery at the end of the coaxial cable had reached the South Pole of the binary. Capsules on tank-treads split along their lateral axes and their tops reared back like clamshells; some extended derricks before and counterweights behind; some blossomed with petals that were tungsten-carbide dozer blades. They attacked an immemorial junk pile, gently prying or fiercely ramming as need was. They burrowed through holed and oxidized piping, tangled old convection plates from ancient heat-exchanger apparatus, the lead jacket of an obsolete thorium reactor, the cans of thorium themselves, the scrapped cylinder of a relatively small fusion reactor and the tumbled heaps of cer-met bricks which once had jacketed it.

They came to a vaulted wall beneath the rubble; oxyhydrogen blowpipes drilled at it, and the mining machinery inserted and tamped explosive charges. No danger of damaging what was within; sonar said it was a dozen HE blasts to the other side. The explosive blew, and sheared off slices; the catspaws of the machines swept them aside. Eleven times more the tamp-blast-and-sweep cycle, and then delicate drilling, and then the hole-through into a chamber the duplicate of that at the North Pole, but with no blue-green monster under a crystal dome.

Instead, there were books.

Circular crystal plates with gold symbols

plated onto them, the plates not bound but
merely stacked together with blessed ineffi-
ciency; the golden text was raised a little, so
the stacked plates did not fit snugly together.
The books were heaped and tumbled on
shelves, tables and the floor. It was a warm
sight absorbed by the image-orthicon eyes,
pulsed back along the coaxial cable, displayed
to the sixteen eyes of the Snowflake on a round
television screen.

The Snowflake gazed, coldly understanding,
on the warm sight and some of its hands clicked
out messages to manipulating machines at the
end of its seventy-six geographic degrees of
coaxial arm. Metal fingers spread the crystal-
and-gold pages, the largest set of pages logically first. The beautiful strange letters ran
unbroken in a spiral from the rim of each plate
to the center, with the logic of boustrophedon
writing, the ancient first-to-the-right-then-to-
the-left lines that somehow lost out to the
system which demanded a break and wrench
of the eyes at the end of each line. The Snowflake noted the nature of the "ink and paper;"
it was not accidental. They were chosen for
the highest possible contrast. The color contrast was absolute; the plates were transparent
and the text opaque. They contrasted in tactility;
the plates were smooth and the gold was grainy,
unburnished. Instruments told the Snowflake
that the contrast in conductivity was as extreme; the plates were insulators and the symbols superconductive. The messages left there

at the South Pole had been left to be read by
almost any eyes, any hands, or whatever
unimaginable beings might read by electricity.
There had to be a key, and there was: on the
set of largest plates.

A wearying, difficult, often-imagined program began. A single man of Earth could eventually have learned much of what was on the
largest plates; it began with arithmetic—of
course, binary. A dot is a dot; a dot and a
space are two dots. Two dots are three dots;
their zero was really zero—nothing, a discon-
tinuity in the flowing script. A gracious, subtly-
curved eye-shape was the addition-operator;
negative numbers were made not of dots but
little sun-bursts, and so on. It was only mathematics; the Snowflake plowed deliberately
through it all, kid-stuff geometry, the functions of the conic sections. It was not very
elegant; the Snowflake felt that elegance had
been foregone and crude old concepts resur-
rected from primitive days. But the Snowflake
learned; this is "height" sign, this is "skill"
sign, "big," "bigger than," "includes," "logically implies"—and then on to the first reader,
the second-largest of the sets of plates. Blue-
green, tentacled monsters were the subjects;
eating, sleeping, crawling (but say "walking")
were the verbs. Monsters (but say "men") watch
the stars. The great sun rises and warms men.
The spermatiferous man impregnates ("loves?")
the ovipositing man—whom you might as
well call a woman, for she is. For one hundred

and sixty-six days the laid egg is—it certainly seemed to be *worshipped*. Then the child is born, and the second degree of worship is accorded to it. A small— Something—is assigned to the child, and the child is cleansed with the mouths of its—certainly not "impregnating" here; certainly "loving" —parents. The child eats good food under the guidance of its parents and its Something-again. The child sleeps too heavily and the Something-again wakes its parents who in loving concern do something about it, the Snowflake could not make out what. The child learns to count and to read books like this. The modified-loving Something-again helps. The child walks, the child runs in the sun, the child goes far and fast riding the Something-again, for the Something-again has grown with the child. Then the child is half-grown and the third degree of worship is accorded to it and it begins to master the Twelve Hundred and Eighteen Books of First Importance. When that is done the child is grown and is a child no longer but a man or woman, and its Something-again too is grown. The new-grown man is modified-loving to the full-grows Something-again, for there is a certain danger in Somethings-again, useful in everything though they are. Absent-mindedness in the treatment ("tentaculation"—"handling") of a full-grown Something-again can be fatal—

The Snowflake quivered in its nutrient bath when it realized that absent-mindedness had been fatal. The full-grown Pyramids, conve-

nient things to have around, had risen immemorial ages ago and destroyed their masters
who had built them, gutted their pleasant planet
and turned it into a bleak junkpile, a fit environment for the machines they were.

15

As Haendl had grimly foreseen, the human beings in the vast corridor of the machine shop next were deprived of their water. The taps simply stopped running.

There was panic, as might have been predicted, and then there was the inevitable consequence: migration. Men with flesh on them do not lie down to die; women with babies in them do not despair. If they are ringed by fire they will break through where the flames seem thinnest, but they will break through. With hunger at their heels and nothing worse than hunger ahead, men go anywhere: from the ancestral home in the Indus Valley or the Euphrates or the Congo they eat their way across the old world, then cross a land bridge and eat their way down the new.

These migrants spread out from the corridor through its two exits; they scouted the red-lit caverns of the binary, twenty, forty miles a day. They found water everywhere, for it is a useful solvent and took part in most of the mechanized planet's chemical processing. They bashed many a pipe loose from its joints and drank their fill and spread on. Scent guided them one hundred miles before they looked again like sober Citizens, ribs countable and thighs dwindling into stringy shanks; but by then they were in the metabolic-products complex of the binary, a tangle of pipes, pumps and vats many of which held sugars, starches, proteins and fats.

Epics should be written about Innison and how he scaled the hundred-foot fermentation tank where glucose was going over into alcohol, and how he shattered the glass input main so that food showered down upon the throng below. Nor should be forgotten The Tale of Muhandas Dutta, and How He Blew up the Polyethelene Cooker. The vast thing stood between them and an unmistakable meaty, yeasty odor. They were abounding with energy from the glucose but their bodies knew they were starving for replacement and repair molecules, that they could not live on energy alone. Princeton Wolves studied the stages of the polyethelene tower, a glum stainless-steel citadel from which protruded clear blisters filled with the successive polymers. Down at the bottom, swirling gas only; heat and pressure filled the next higher blister with thin fluid, and the blister above with viscous fluid, and up at the top great paddles churned a waxy paste through the output main to a storage facility or direct to presses and extrusion nozzles which might be half a world away. A planetful of circuitry was always in need of some insulation, somewhere; shorts were spitting blue fire somewhere at any given moment, and machines crawling toward them laden with copper and polyethelene pellets to stop the bleeding and heal the wounds. And this source of dressings stood like a bastion between the men and the smell of yeast. There was no way around except through vats of fuming nitric acid, rooms whose air was death.

Muhandas Dutta consulted with Wolves, warned all the others back around solid walls and onto high ground up ramps, and alone climbed a great, rugged weld that led half-way up the fermentation tank. There was the place where ethanol was drawn off, and there it was tasted by instruments whose wires led somehere to a Component. The end of the wires that mattered to Dutta went through a packing gland into the output main. The gland was strong, but it was not homogeneous with the rest of the tank and pipe. There were places where the gland and the pipe met, and there Dutta inserted his milling-machine sliver and pried. With one arm and both legs he clung to the meter-thick pipe; with the other he pried for an hour, two hours, three hours. When scouts came wandering from around the thick walls where he had sent them he screamed down at them to go back; it was giving way. So the scouts returned to the people, and the people waited, hungry and thirsty, smashing water pipes for their drink, getting out of the way of slow-moving pipe-repair machines when they came, and smashing the pipes again when they were gone.

In the fourth hour of Dutta's ordeal the packing gland started to sweat ethanol drops at its edges. In the fifth hour came a dribbling stream whose fumes made him cling dizzily, and in the sixth the gland blasted out like a bullet and blew Muhandas Dutta with it, destroying him like a mutineer blown from the muzzle of a gun.

The ethanol roared down in a glassy column to the floor, and sped downgrade to the polyethelene cooker's cherry-red base. The ethanol boomed into blue flame on contact, and the cherry-red of the cooker went into orange-red and then orange. The explosion ripped it an instant later, puffing out all flame with a gigantic breath. Distracted repair machines sprinkled the hot rubble and pawed at riven plates. When their fire-control fluid stopped sizzling on the tangled wreckage the human beings came out and climbed it, threading around fantastic spires and hummocks of polychome plastic extruded before its time and untimely chilled; from the top of the heap they could see the promised land: flat culture tanks of yeast indefatigably working away under arc lights, manufacturing proteins, handy, versatile long-chain molecules, and nutritious, too.

For the time being, their food problem was solved. To solve it they had done the binary planet a century's-worth of damage in a matter of hours; they were being excellent mice.

Through the Snowflake quivered the realization that this was a problem beyond intellect: what ought one to think of entities-that-were-machines instead of entities-that-were-living? Logic alone could make no distinction. On a gross level there was oh, what difference between a lever and a poet! But logic did not stop with levers and poets. Logic went on to consider the difference between a self-programming computer and the microscopically-revealed network of electro-chemical feedback processes that could grossly be called "a poet," and found the difference smaller. And logic could not be stopped from going on to machines unbuilt, the most complex machine imaginable, capable of choice, self-reproducing, versatile with limbs and transducers, and comparing it with a description unwritten, the most exhaustive description of "a poet" that could be produced, bearing in mind that there was really nothing in him but input, switching and output. On the nameplate of a machine and on the brow of a poet might be inscribed with equal justice *Ex Nihil Nihil Fit;* you get nothing from nothing. You get bombarded by the environment with sense-impressions and something happens, machine or man. You input a pound of force on the long end of a three-to-one lever; it outputs three pounds (over a shorter distance). You input travel books on Samuel Taylor Coleridge; he outputs Xanadu. So simple!

So wrong. The Snowflake fluttered in its tank knowing it was wrong, but not why or how. It decided (a rare decision) to dissociate into its eight personalities for a time.

It was harder than ever before for Glenn Tropile. It wrenched him and gave him the curious illusion that he had gone blind—even though his own two eyes could see the murk of the nutrient fluid, his own deformed toenail, the tangle of wires and the switches in his pink, wrinkled hands. Have to adjust the salt content of the nutrient, he thought. There whipped through his mind frighteningly the ion-exchange equations that explained the wrinkling—a hang-over of the endlessly analytical life within the Snowflake.

Django Tembo of course spoke first. "Children," he said, "the last of my hesitation is gone. I have no more compassion for these invaders, the Pyramids; they were bad servants and rebels. This can never be tolerated. It must be war to the death." For the Snowflake had considered a *modus vivendi* with the Pyramids as perhaps the most economical solution of the problem.

There was a soundless murmur of agreement.

"What place this?" Willy asked, and began to cry.

"Hush, Willy," Mercedes van Dellen soothed him. "It's all right. We're your friends." Willy put his thumb in his mouth, not letting go of his switch, and was at peace. *Warm here. Good here.*

It was, surprisingly, Kim Seong who spoke up next: "We should have a little talk with the fellow under the North Pole, the green boy with all the arms. He's older than any of us."

"He's dead!" Tropile said, astonished.

"Must be nice to be so cocksure," she said dryly. "I, of course, wouldn't know, not being a man. All *I* know is that it's smart to be ready for any dirty little trick that can be sprung on you."

Alla Narova said: "I think they're sorry they killed all their people. I think they're trying to revive that one; that's what all the puttering is about. I think they want to tell it they're sorry."

"No, no!" cried Corso Navarone. "You are too forgiving in your womanly heart. They are fiends; they are tormenting it. Death to the monsters, I say, and I shall say it forever!" If he could have folded his arms he would have, but the wire-trailing switches got in the way.

Spyros Gulbenkian said: "Let us consider the whole situation, my friends. We should hit them high and hit them low. Our hitting low proceeds successfully; our good people from Earth have provided the repair-machines with tasks of an order of magnitude beyond their programming or mechanical capacities. Soon several score of the women will come to term. The second generation, my dear friends! Let them only grow to sexual maturity in thirteen or fourteen clock-years and this planet is doomed! But I am overdramatic. The earth-people will multiply, I should say, and the pyramids and their machinery will fail to cope with them. Time is on our side—what a luxury for an old man to say that! Misunderstood, un-understood, they will proliferate through the planet in their innocent way. They will drain sedimentation pans to establish new yeast beds unmindful that sediment-laden coke pellets will produce quite inferior steel with which the Pyramids will order devices to be manufactured. They will notice that a chamber is quite livable as to temperature and humidity except that chlorine gas is blown through it. In their innocence they will jam the fan which drives the chlorine, not knowing or caring that this lack of chlorine will end for a time the production on this planet of polychloroprene without which oil-resistant gaskets cannot be manufactured. The weak flesh! The weak flesh, driven by hunger and progeny! What wreckage the weak flesh will do to iron-bound machines!"

"I won't wait a century," Tropile snarled.

"For what?" asked Gulbenkian, blandly.

"For—for—" He did not know. He said almost as a question: "To be human again. Walk the Earth . . . my God, *what are we doing*?"

Willy began to cry with fright. Mercedes van Dellen soothed him.

"What are we doing?" Tropile asked again, trying to be calm. "We've ripped our friends out of the Earth and turned them loose to be vermin for our convenience. We weren't a god; we were a devil!"

Like the flip of a kaleidoscope events had suddenly changed while he watched them. The steady certainty of the Snowflake which knew nothing except tasks and their economical fulfillment had become the inhuman fixity of a machine.

"We were a machine!" he cried. "We were as much a machine as the Pyramids. There was no soul in us, no pity."

"Yes," said Alla Narova, suddenly awed. "How could we have done it? Django Tembo, how could you have *let* us?"

The dung-bearer had the soul of a king—but an African king. Deeply troubled, he told them: "Look into my heart and you will see why I do not understand your objections."

They looked and saw. He had been fundamentally baffled by "not a god but a devil." To him it had sounded like the crudest, most naked illogic. Devil and god were the same to his people after millenia in fatless, acid-soiled Africa. Men do not eat other men calmly except in Africa. Siberian shamans used to tear madly at the flesh of those who watched them dance, but every unspeakable mouthful later was vomited up so that the lawbreaking did not bring ruin on the tribe. Polynesians and Melanesians dined on long pig to dare fate and trembled when they did it. Only in starved Africa was a man the same as meat, no more and no less. So it was that when Tropile spoke, Django Tembo heard him say: "We weren't a devil-god; we were a devil-god." He could not understand that as a value-judgment; nobody could.

Gulbenkian chuckled at the impasse.

Django Tembo said, puzzled and simple: "Strength is better than weakness, friends. Together we are strong. What more is there to say? Who can guide every step so that no ant is ever crushed by him?"

"You'll never get me back in there," said Tropile.

"Or me," said Alla Narova.

"You cannot do this!" Corso Navarone cried. "Alla Narova whom I love, Glen Tropile, my trusted companion, deserters? Never!"

"I think the same," said Spyros Gulbenkian with interest. "I mean *really* think, with the brain and not with the gonads—no offense, Corso. Exactly how are you going to desert? I think we can, so to speak, pull you under if we wish."

"Try it!" Tropile snarled.

"Try it!" Alla Narova echoed.

"If it weren't for Willy," Mercedes van Dellen said apologetically. "He'd be lost without us—"

Kim Seong said delightedly: "I'll just watch. I love a good fight between a pair of fools. It breaks things up."

Tropile and Alla Narova felt the attack begin from Django Tembo; it came in the form of false memories insinuating themselves into their minds. Glaring deserts of rock and sand that merged into snowy steppes, the death of the last elephant, on Earth, Tembo's totem, in the streets of Durban, the aged ivory-laden beast crashing to its arthritic knees and toppling on its side, grunting . . . Princeton and Gala dimmed in Tropile's mind, Nice, and the old blind man in Alla Narova's. The fierce, confused, inflated thoughts of Corso Navarone exhorted them to be brave, strong, united, gallant, dignified like *him*. Spyros Gulbenkian, never one to lead a cavalry charge, spattered them with this day in Paris six sun-cycles ago when he won the toll-gate franchise on the Ninth Bridge, the foundation of his fortune; that night in Frankfurt's House of Regulations when he blew the wall and permitted his chief bookkeeper to escape—the charge was Wolf, of course; an afternoon between the paws of the Great Sphinx when he and a trader named Shalom bartered African grain for French sugarbeet. Mercedes van Dellen: *Poor Willy. He doesn't really understand but he feels better when we're all together. He forgets that he doesn't understand. Maybe he's improving. Don't you think so? Maybe the next time we come out he'll be a little clearer. Wouldn't that be good? Glen and Alla, won't you let go for poor Willy?*

And Alla Narova broke the flashing exchange with an angry sob. "Willy's upset!" she cried. "He won't answer me."

With an effort, Tropile expelled the false memories and the pseudo-voices. "Stop a minute, everybody!" he shouted. "If you're so worried about what Willy wants, let's give him a chance to speak for himself."

The Snowflake—seven-eighths of it—fell silent. It was the turn of the remaining one-eighth to speak.

It didn't do so, however. Uncertainly, Alla Narova quavered, "Willy?"

No answer.

"He feels *funny*," said Spyros Gulbenkian.

Then everybody knew that Willy felt funny, because the motionless body jerked into violent motion. "What's he doing?" Tropile cried. "Willy! Cut it out! The way you're wriggling around you could hurt something!"

The suddenly thrashing, sinuously writhing body of Willy became motionless again. Then, member by member, systematically it moved a finger at a time, a toe, an arm, like the owner of a new car trying out its controls.

"My God," breathed Mercedes van Dellen, "it's not Willy, is it?"

The voice of Willy said gently, "No. I have borrowed Willy to tell you that you must do something quite soon."

"Willy!" Mercedes screamed.

Willy repeated, "No, not Willy. I'm sorry. I had to kill him, so to speak. He won't be back. I'm what your friend called 'the green boy with all the arms.' "

"Told you so," said Kim Seong.

"Yes, madam," said Willy. "We had your sort in my world, too. It was an interesting world and a pleasant one, at least until we started running it for the benefit of the machines, and then let the machines start running it for their own benefit."

"How can you talk our language?" Corso Navarone asked faintly.

Wistfully Willy said, "We used to have more than two hundred languages, some good for one thing, some good for another. We were expected to know them all. One more—what does it matter? We were a clever race. Oh, yes, we were clever! I have thought for some time that you would be interested to know how clever, ever since I first noticed you observing us."

Mercedes whimpered. "You *noticed?* Did— did the Pyramids also notice?"

"Wait one moment, please," said Willy's voice. There was a lengthy silence. Then Willy's voice said regretfully, "That is something else I would like to talk to you about at some length: What, exactly, do Pyramids 'notice?' But there is something you may think more immediate. You made a mistake when you broke into the Polar Library. You weren't strong enough to do that yet. Of course, you couldn't have been expected to know."

Tropile, awe and shock to one side, had had more than enough of veiled hints and subtle warnings. "So?" he growled.

"So you touched off trouble when you holed through to the Library," Willy said apologetically. "The Pyramids, ah—" It broke off for a moment, then resumed with an almost audible equivalent of a shrug. "Let's say, they 'noticed,' though that is quite inexact. At any rate, the Omniverters—excuse me, what you call the Pyramids—have been waiting to take action for the arrival of the one they keep on your planet. It has arrived. All eight of them are now headed for this tank of yours, with, I believe, the intention of doing a thorough job of destroying it. I wish you well. You are not an unattractive race."

Tropile gritted his teeth; there was nothing veiled or subtle about that; it was all too understandable. "Will you tell us what to do?" he demanded.

"I can't," it said. "I'm dead."

So perhaps it had not been all that understandable after all.

16

There was, of course, no longer any question of personal wishes. Tropile and Alla Narova swiftly slid back into the Snowflake. If they allowed themselves any personal thoughts at that moment, it was only a poignant regret for what might have been. Not an unusual one, in the history of the human race. Their survival was at stake. As good men and women had all through the history of Earth, sometimes in a good cause and sometimes not (though seldom did anyone think it not), they sadly said good-by to reverence for all life, to freedom of speech, to habeas corpus and to the all-too-alienable right to wear striped socks when they chose.

They joined the Army.

They were not, perhaps, a very prepossessing Army, but that didn't matter much; they were definitely at war. They were one significant item in the table of forces deployed on and in the binary planet. There were four altogether:

1, The Snowflake itself (somewhat below strength because one of its members was unavoidably handicapped, being dead.)

2, The other human beings at large somewhere within the planet—the "mice."

And, on the other side of the battle line:

3, The machines and systems of the Pyramids.

4, The Pyramids themselves.

Few human generals would willingly have sought battle when they were so outmatched. The Snowflake didn't seek it either, but the battle was coming nearer to them all the time.

So the Snowflake began to fight. It had long since prepared for the battle—not now, though; not for a long, comfortable time; like most armies at war, it would have been much readier if it had had much more time. It was less ready than it had expected, in fact, because "Willy" was not pulling his weight. Willy was there, all right. They could feel his (or its) presence, observing, appreciating, even sometimes admiring. But the Snowflake was like an eight-engined aircraft with one propeller feathered; it spun uselessly where it should have joined to pull.

That, too, could not be helped, so the Snowflake did what it was able to do. Each member of the seven working ones performed his or her chores. Their hands clicked and rattled the switches, turning on leagues of wire, a dozen generators, a hundred microphones and eyes throughout the binary—the First Approximation Network that gave the Snowflake a quick, dim picture of any overall disturbance. Spy-boxes ranged around the equator told them the eight Pyramids were exactly there, on that imaginary line, equally spaced around the circumference of the planet. The spy boxes further reported that the Pyramids were on the naked jumbled surface of the planet, most unusually, and that from the apex of each there ran to the right and left an inexplicable line which joined all the apexes in a gigantic octagon.

The equatorial spy-boxes died at that moment, and there blasted down the cables from them into the nutrient tank an almost-lethal charge. But the cables vaporized near the equator before the Snowflake could die.

It took minutes to recover and activate a Second Approximation Network, localized now and of finer perception. The Snowflake *saw* the Pyramids then, moving slowly South, and the glaring line that tied them together. It was almost invisible where it streaked through the airless surface; it seared blue-hot where it cut through the curve of the planet before emerging again. Instruments reported to the Snowflake on the nature of the line before they died. The octagon was—or had been—a few pounds of deuterium. It had been heated into raw creation-stuff, hotter than any liquid, solid or gas could be. It was a plasma of raw electrons and deuterons, and the plasma had been shaped into a pencil-thin tubular plasmoid by magnetic fields which the Pyramids emitted. The temperature of the stuff was 100 million degrees and the pressure 22 million pounds per square inch; the particles battering for escape at the magnetic tube confining them were turned suavely aside in a spin at right angles to the field. The particles could not escape; some of their radiant energy could. At 100 million degrees continuous fusion went on within the plasmoid, releasing energy on a solar scale. As the octagonal girdle about the planet moved slowly southward, all the steel it met puddled and ran; all the copper it crossed puffed away, vaporized. The remote eyes of the Snowflake began to wink out in death. It was plain that the Pyramids were erasing half of their planet to keep the other half.

It was plain that the southern hemisphere was being made uninhabitable for everything that the Pyramids understood: wires, relays, generators, electron tubes, transistors, thermistors, spacistors, transformers and whatever depended utterly on them. Connections were being broken; networks were ceasing to function; life as they knew it—and that included Components and the Snowflake—would become extinct.

Life as they did not know it went on.

Roget Germyn toasted yeast cakes over a small fire—alcohol in a wrenched-off grease cup, wicked-up by insulating fiber from a hot pipe. Alcohol was abundant, but nobody ever drank it now. Drinking it one never knew whether it was ethanol or methanol until three days later. Then, if it had been methanol, one went blind and died. This confusion between the benign alcohol and its deadly cousin had taken off a dozen reckless men and women. His tribe had shrunk all told by fifty per cent; a few heroes like Muhandas Dutta were dead, and the rest had been weaklings of one kind or another, people who couldn't go five days without food and water, people who stuffed themselves with dubious yeasts because they didn't taste too wrong, people who couldn't climb walls, jump gaps, keep from stumbling into naked bus bars, people who grieved to death for rice or wife or sunset clouds.

Roget Germyn was too busy to grieve, so he lived on, no theorist, not very cerebral, but glorying in a full gut, in taking a strong woman, in waking and lying extra minutes idly on a bed of polyurethane foam raped from its cushioning job in a stamping mill. He considered himself Third in Command, after Haendl and Innison, and so did everybody else.

Big Chief Haendl joined him at the fire, carrying a thermoplastic scrap heated and dented into a bucket. It was full of colorless fluid, and the fire was running low. Germyn automatically went through a routine of dipping thumb and forefinger into the fluid, rubbing them together, raising them to his nose to sniff, and touching them to his tongue. It took only a half-second and it was one of the things survival depended on. The subconscious decision was: It's all right; it won't put out the fire and also it won't explode in our faces. He nodded to Haendl and Haendl poured the fluid carefully into the grease cup; the blue flame burned higher from the white tufted wicking and the hand-patted yeast cakes sizzled on their wire spit. Haendl was now entitled to one of them when they were done through.

Haendl said: "Maybe this is the last of the alcohol."

"How?"

"I busted a pipe at the joint and caught my bucketful. A machine started to crawl over, then it began to *spin*."

"I never saw one of them do that."

"No. Then the machine stopped. Dead. The motor stopped turning. Then the alcohol stopped running from the pipe."

The binary was not a quiet place. Usually within earshot there was heavy machinery doing things that produced a background rumble. As they sat and shared the cakes the rumble intensified. They did not leap up or even speak, but went on chewing. In the past months those who survived had learned not to waste energy on anything except survival. All through the yeast-pan chamber they occupied, three hundred or so ex-Citizens took minimum notice and continued to eat, sleep, harvest the pans, shape their cakes, build their fires, make their tools of scraps and broken parts.

The daylight lamps used by the yeast for photosynthesis went out abruptly and there were cries of fright until eyes accommodated to the dim light of chemically luminous ceiling panels.

Then came heat. The North wall began to glow—sooty red, brighter orange, lemon-yellow, blue, blue-white—and a thing like a hot wire stretching the length of the room emerged from it and moved at a walking pace above their heads. The opposite wall blazed blue-white as the plasmoid vanished into it and then there was silence except for a diminishing rumble to the south. It soon dampened into nothingness.

The ceiling panels glowed down unchanged on yeast pans which had been boiled dry, on plastic which had melted and dribbled, and on three hundred sprawled, silent figures. One by one they began to stir and look up. Some were temporarily blinded; all suffered angry red first-degree burns, but no radiation sickness. Fusion is hot and clean. Dazedly they pulled themselves up on the edges of the yeast pans to look over into their dry charred depths. One by one they turned their backs on the vanishing planetary rumble and moved draggingly North. They were hungry and there was no food on the site or to the South, so they went North. They were life as the Pyramids did not know it, so they had passed through the Pyramids' *cordon sanitaire*, as the Snowflake never could.

The Snowflake retreated. It had its escape tunnel to the surface, and it crawled up the slanting tunnel on caterpillar treads. It was by then the heart of an immense complex: armor, reserve nutrient, circulation pumps, power sources for the pumps and its far-reaching sense organs and manipulators. It was, in fact, the size of a Pyramid, though not as mobile. It emerged to the surface and continued its slow crawl southward, skirting junkpiles, circling crevasses. The two nerve trunks it maintained were: a feeder to a simple eye-and-ear up North which observed the progress of the octagonal cordon; and: the line to the South where manipulators dealt out crystal-and-gold plates in the polar library to be read by the Snowflake's eyes.

The difficulty, of course, was that the Snowflake's eyes had learned to read only one of the two hundred languages of the old green boys with all the arms. Worse than that, the plates were tumbled in random order.

Within the Snowflake, Glenn Tropile cursed. "What do we do now?" he demanded of no one in particular.

"We sort them out," Alla Narova said strongly. "We can't fight what we don't understand."

"It will take forever," complained Gulbenkian. "We don't have forever."

Alla Narova flashed, "Let us consider. Why are the plates scattered? There must be a system. That first, then. We deduce the system, then—"

"Then," said Tropile bitterly, "we still can't read the damned things. Anyway, who says there has to be a system? Suppose the green people had some sort of precognitive ability?

Then whichever plate they reached for would be the right one—so why make card indexes?"

And Willy said admiringly, "You really are quite clever, you know. We did."

"Willy!" cried Alla Narova. "What do we do now?"

Willy said with regret, "I'm really sorry, but, as I am d—"

"Hell with your being dead!" said Tropile brutally. "Can you at least help us read these damn things?"

"Well, certainly I can do *that*," said the voice, slightly miffed. "One moment. There."

And the crystal and gold rearranged itself into texts, as two hundred languages flowed into the Snowflake net. "My God," whispered Tropile, marveling. "Willy? Now can you tell us which of these—"

"But that wouldn't be fair," said Willy seriously, "under the circumstances."

So the Snowflake began to devour the library. The first book it spun under the television eyes was promising: *Treatise on Strategy for the Use of [Unintelligible]*. Strategy! The Snowflake read the book in five minutes. Strategy turned out to be in the nature of a white cane and a Seeing Eye Dog—something to be used by unfortunate green people whom accident or illness had deprived of telepathy. The doctrine of gambits, planned withdrawals and encirclement was the very latest in prosthetic devices. Those crystal and gold plates went crashing into a corner of the chamber; the busy fingers plucked and burrowed into the pile again.

Mathematical Aesthetics of First-Stage Egg-Worship. Five minutes to read; nothing there except an old seven-based notation traditional to the rites, and: "—our inevitable human tendency to polarize which we have impressed even on our machines—"

Impregnation as an Art Form. (It ranked below Spacio-Temporal, Electromagnetic Constructs, and well above Precognition Capping—but only as an art form. It was clearly understood that as a noncerebral experience it was second only to the supreme one, Willed Death.)

The Pre-Machine Culture of [some planet of some star]. Amusing little beggars; one envied their simplicity, to say nothing of their low accident rate.

Is Polarity an Artifact? Well, yes—which was a polar way of putting it. In the raw universe as distinguished from the universe ordered by the mind of man there was no polarity. Yet the universe itself had given rise by evolution to the polar mind of man with its on-or-off nerve cells, man's informing eyes which decided things were either light or dark rather than taking an accurate photon count. The universe suffered itself to be arranged into abstractions manipulable by dyadic notation with its implicit duality. In meta-language—

The meta-language was almost unintelligble, and was only an introduction to a totally unintelligible treatment in meta-meta-language.

Architecture for People and their Omniverters. This golden (actually "palladian"—they loved the hard black-silvery sheen of Element 46 more than the fatty texture of gold) age of leisure and creativity . . . new and challenging . . . traditional and seven-based aesthetic of ovoids must either yield or graciously blend with the new demands of superbly versatile machinery . . . the Omniverter the flower of the mechanical genius of our race . . . some compromise essential for aesthetic unity . . . widening of roads beyond any degree hitherto contemplated lest traffic be choked . . . Omniverter shelter-feeding-booth for every impregnation-group . . . hoped that accommodations rationally and beautifully arranged for the almost-symbiotic life of man and his machinery will minimize the accident rate hitherto considered the inevitable consequence of progress . . .

Omniverter Safety Book. The Omniverter is non-reasoning despite its astonishing versatility. The Seventh Conference on Omniverter Safety has concluded that failure to recognize this fact and act appropriately is the basis of the high and rising accident rate. It has even been somewhat blasphemously suggested that Second-Stage Egg-Worship Ritual be altered to include basic techniques of Omniverter safety in order to emphasize the gravity of the problem . . .

Omniverter Ideation: a Debate. Pro—the characteristic polar behavior of all Omniverters. They invariably lay out a job of work by setting the limits and filling in between them, whether it is to build a feeding-station factory or a road-widening machine. *Con*—this is merely a mechanical consequence of the binary concepts underlying their construction (Both very much elaborated.) Chairman's humorous conclusion—unfortunately we cannot ask an Omniverter whether this characteristic is associated with the idea of polarity or is a mere reflex. Therefore we stand adjourned.

Rise and Fall of the Omniverter Movement: Omniverters—Pyramids—the definitive history! Ten minutes to read it. Simple solid-state physics devices with many advantages over fragile, hot-running electron tubes. Bigger and bigger, better and better. The inevitable dream of robots; make 'em *really* big, one fine solid jam of transistors switching busily away, running factories, feeding themselves, healing themselves, tending the young—fellows and girls, we've got it made! *This* is living; we have leisure to make bigger and better Omniverters for everybody, to ride on Omniverters instead of walking, to tear up farmland for germanium and caesium to make bigger and better Omniverters. We never had it so good, except for the inevitable Omniverter accidents, which are merely the toll taken by progress; indeed there is a growing body of evidence that people accidentally injured *want* the accidents to happen to them so (somehow) we needn't do anything about it.

Somebody whose name was spelled with a sunburst, a teapot spout, a pineapple shape and an H shape proved that the accidents weren't accidents but murders. Everybody thought he was crazy until three Omniverters hewed their way through his elaborate defenses to get him.

The green people were not fools. There was an instant, planetwide embargo against Omniverters at great cost in convenience and even hunger. All Omniverter feeding-stations were thoroughly wrecked; one by one the sullen machines slowed down, stopped and were dismantled. The world reconverted with aching muscles; all was well; every recorded Omniverter was accounted for except the eight Specials built for interplanetary exploration and long, long gone, presumed lost by a plunge into the sun—

"Willy!" Tropile cried. "Those eight missing Pyramids—?"

Mournfully Willy's voice said, "Yes. That is right. They came back."

And because they came back, the next chapter of that book was never written. The eight Specials had returned without warning. Brutishly they perceived that there were no feeding stations, that they were under attack, that there were no other Omniverters on the planet but them. They then proceeded to wipe out the people with beams of electrons, hot plasmoids and direct pressure. When this was done they built their own feeding stations in plenty of time, and then built devices to serve the feeding stations, and devices to serve those devices until the final irony was achieved of men wired together to serve machines. The Pyramids were human enough never to leave well enough alone, and human enough to preserve a place which was *fas*, lucky, lawful, all good things, at the North Pole, and a place which was *nefas*, dangerous, feared, at the South. And the dangerous place was truly dangerous; it had concealed the clue of the feeding stations.

These great three-sided booths on the equator then were the be-all and end-all of the planetful of junk. On them focused the pipes of the metabolic-products area. On them focused the propulsion machinery that moved the planet. On them focused the impedimenta surrounding the fleet of space ships which renewed the Sun. On them focused the planning and programming machinery and Components that assessed and allocated demands for power and materials from the competing systems.

The Snowflake's television eye to the North reported that the octagon had snapped off briefly and been replaced by an irregular heptagon—a Pyramid was feeding. In their delousing operation, how could a split second matter? But it did; one of the spiderspies, almost mindlessly waiting, programmed not to destroy itself, scuttled South during the moment between octagon and heptagon when blue flame did not bar its path. Gratefully it made for the television cable, plugged itself in and discharged its magnetic memory. Its dispatch was: the human beings have survived; I saw them live through the heat and go North.

"So there it is," said Spyros Gulbenkian, his voice shaking.

"There it is," agreed Alla Narova. The problem and the solution, they were all there.

Said Django Tembo, "Which one of us shall go?" It was a shorthand kind of question. What it stood for was, *The only way for us to fight now is for one of us to physically separate from the Snowflake and make the trip in his physical person.* And what *that* meant by "physically separate" was *Give up our indissoluble, ineluctable, indispensable unity forever.* Nor would the separation be any physically easier than the surgical joining had been in the first place.

"It's my job," said Tropile bitterly. "There are more of my people than anyone else's, the Princeton bunch being what they were. It's time to let them at the 'copter and the explosives. It's time they had a leader who knew what he was doing. Call in the sawbones machine."

The words cost him what it would cost an ordinary mind to pull the trigger of a pistol fatally aimed, or to let go of a mountain ledge. They did not dispute with him, though one-seventh of them was dying.

The neurosurgery machine, all glittering metal hands, which had united them was part of their massive complex of equipment. A tube from it slipped into his nostrils, bubbling gas that dosed him against pain. He mumbled an agonized farewell before sleep closed down on him, the first sleep he had known since his awakening six months ago.

What was left of Willy told what was left of the Snowflake: "I can't do much, but I can keep him in contact with you until—"

"We thank you," the Snowflake said. "Do not be embarrassed for us."

The mind of the green and tentacled monster rippled uneasily. "You're inhuman," it complained. "Still, to settle the old grudge . . ."

"We understand."

17

The tribe was patched and blistered, and greased its wounds with glycerine. Before stumbling into the northern sector of the metabolic-products area they had resorted to a horrible expedient for survival. Starving, they came to a computer center that was hundreds of human bodies in individual tanks of fluid; wires came from the temples. Some of the bodies they recognized—a cousin here, a Rice Master there. One of the few surviving born fools among them cracked a tank and sipped fluid from his cupped hands, and they let him. He did not die, so like the savages they were, they fell to and drained the tanks. The nutrient fluid fed them and rebuilt their seared tissues astonishingly. It was gone in a clock-day, but they moved on refreshed, not choosing to think of what they had left in the dry tanks. And a clock-day later they were reestablished in another yeast bay, had identified water and alcohol mains, and were living again.

The stranger who lurched into the big arc-lit room a day later was not at once identifiable. He was burned as badly as any of them; women screamed when they saw him, thinking that he must be a—a Something from one of the violated nutrient tanks.

But he kept mumbling through cracked lips: "Tropile. Want Haendl. Innison. Germyn." They brought Haendl to him.

"Tropile," the Wolf said, studying him. "Do you want me to send for your wife?"

"Wife?" the burnt man muttered. "We have no wife. Follow me. Us. Me."

"You're raving. We can't follow a delirious man," Haendl said soothingly. "Rest a few days; we have, ah, some stuff to help you heal—"

"Fetch it. We'll use it on the march. We propose to lead you to your weapons." He looked straight into Haendl's eyes.

The man from Princeton passed his hand in front of his face. "Tropile! You *are* Tropile? I thought—I don't know what I thought." He said harshly over his shoulder to Innison and Germyn: "Well? You heard him, didn't you? Get the people together."

Afterwards, long afterwards, he tried to explain: "It was like six people challenging you to a fist fight—six of them to one of you. Of course you don't take them up on it; you'd be crazy if you did. I wasn't crazy, so I didn't challenge Tropile's right to take over."

They strung yeast-cakes to themselves, wincing where they touched burns, and followed their sick, crazy-sounding messiah out of the warm, bright yeast bay into cold, or sweltering-hot, tunnels where the air was too thin, or too thick, or acrid with fumes. Gala Tropile was one of the marchers; she refused for days to believe that the man was Glen. He looked something like Glen but he did not know her; the most she would finally concede was that he was Glen Tropile *in a way*. What had happened to him was unguessable. She thought vaguely that he might be made well if she could comfort him and kiss the queer scars, not burns, on his forehead.

Their leader never hesitated; they reeled off a steady forty miles per day. When he took them into a chamber that was 140 degrees of desiccated heat, it turned out to be exactly possible to cross it without collapsing. When he nerved them for a dash through a spectro-photometry room chilled to space-cold for the desired superconductivity effect the weakest of them could just live through the two dozen terrible steps.

It was from one of those cold rooms that they burst into the bottom of a huge well, open to the black star-studded sky except for a glass roof to contain the thin air. It had been a photo-observatory, but now the mirror, photon multipliers, spectroscope gratings and interferometers were crushed under sudden new arrivals of equipment. This was an arsenal now, the Princeton arsenal transferred to the binary. Guns, explosives, a tank, the war helicopter, rations, body armor, respirators, tank after tank of oxygen for the aborted attack on Everest.

Haendl and Innison inventoried the weapons happily, crooned over demolition bombs, land mines and four-point-two mortars. Tropile stood like a television camera on "pan," his head moving slowly back and forth, scanning the scene. He said at last: "Paper and pencil." His hand went out like a hydraulic actuator and waited, without fatigue, until the paper and pencil were brought. He flicked his hand over the paper and it was a smoothly-drawn map; the lines were *drafted*, as if he had paused after each to twist the pencil point against a sanding block, and as if they had been guided by T-square, triangles and french curves. In a second pass down the paper he lettered in designations, instructions and routes, and handed the sheet to Haendl. He reached for another. Two passes and the second map was ready for Innison. And then the third for Germyn. And a dozen more for platoon leaders, and three dozen more for squad leaders.

He did not make a Plutarchian before-the-battle address to his gallant troops; he just waited, looking turned-off, while his commanders studied the maps.

At length it was time. The Snowflake, crawling South on its caterpillar treads, flashed the thought to what lay under the crystal dome, and from there it was relayed to Tropile. The Snowflake, receiving its acknowledgement, reversed its left-hand tread, rotated 180 degrees, and began crawling north towards the girdle of fire. The cordon was then a pentagon; reliefs for feeding had become very frequent as the Pyramids steadily drained their energy out in maintaining the colossal magnetic field needed to hold the plasmoid. Signals from the five on the firing line to the three at the feeding booths—signals without agitation or emotion. The three broke off feeding and began to glide across the tumbled planetary surface southward to join the cordon, maximize its intensity.

"The feeding stations are abandoned," Tropile said dryly. "We will move to them following our maps. Explosives will be detonated as shown. All breaches in primary food lines will be defended against repair machinery."

The primary food lines. The ragged tribe from Earth could not now be likened to mice which nibbled at the superficies of a building; they had become wolves, going for the throat of the dweller.

They moved out, guided by the man who was guided by the Snowflake and the green, tentacled, suffering thing under the crystal dome up North. The arms cache was located one mile from the feeding booths which stood like basalt cliffs along the equator. In full Everest gear they ascended to the surface through a slanting tunnel and fanned out in nine groups for a mile of hard mountaineering across the junkpile world. Eight of the groups worked their way toward the booths, specifically toward the points where each booth was penetrated by a pipe twenty-five feet in diameter, made of extruded half-inch steel. The ninth group under Germyn and Tropile made for the huger pipe which emerged from the heart of the metabolics-complex, surfaced, and then subdivided into the eight booth mains.

They did their usual rodent damage as they went.

One stepped on a low-tension wire strung inches from the floor of the slanting tunnel; the wire broke. A low-priority message went out: wire broken. A repair machine on routine patrol noted the fact, and checked its magazine to see whether it had voltage and amperage enough to patch in the break, enough polyethelene pellets to squeeze an insulating jacket over the patch. Then the machine either headed for a supply station or to the break, and fixed it. Average time for such a repair, about an hour.

One of the tribe was thirsty and performed what had become a reflex action to thirst. She identified a water pipe by a hundred subtle signs that made it different from all other pipes—temperature, material, finish, gradient, position. She broke it at a joint and trudged on, leaving it running from the break. A higher-priority message went out: pressure-drop; water pipe broken. A quicker machine came to weld it; water on the loose caused shorts, rotting, snowballing trouble. It was not much of a machine; if it came while you drank and stupidly tried to push you aside and weld the pipe you could hold it off at arm's length while its treads spun and it reached foolishly for the pipe. Time for arrival averaged fifteen minutes.

There was a rule: when a pipe obviously contained the products of several pipes, when it was a Y or a *psi* or a nameless figure of many more branches and only a single outlet, you were careful. If you broke the stem of a fixture like that, special repair machines came fast, and big. The more branches, the faster they came, and the bigger they were, and the more determined. You could barely hold off with both hands the squat little tri-wheeled plumber that came to repair a broken Y joint. Two men could not restrain the half-ton thing that came rushing to restore a broken *psi*.

More than once the tribe had seen machines booming down the corridors with which they did not care to tangle—high-speed, tread-mounted things weighing up to two tons, equipped with dozer blades and eighteen-inch augers for boring through rubble. It was theorized that they were to service pipes containing something near the end-product of the planet's whole activity, major components of the Pyramid-food.

And they were moving on the food itself.

The Germyn-Tropile group of thirty-odd arrived at their objective. It was a column fifty feet in diameter rising vertically from the summit of a conical slagpile. It soared three times its own diameter into the black sky of the binary and then curved south in a soaring ninety-degree turn. Spidery steel legs supported it every three yards, in pairs. They

could not see its terminus, but knew it ended
in an impregnable sphere from which issued
the eight distribution mains that led directly
into the feeding booths.

Planetary stresses, the bunglings of motile
machines out of control, and fatigue of materials had not spared the riser pipe or the overhead tube. Inevitably, over the aeons, there
had been failures and breakage; their rubble
lay about where the repair-machines had shoved
it. Now and then a pair of legs had crystallized
and snapped, or flowed a little and sagged.
The repair machines had come charging, had
buttressed them, had slapped and welded
patches on the pipe where it was strained. A
huge patch on the riser itself and another exactly opposite it must represent meteor damage repaired. One whole section of fifty-foot
pipe overhead was shinier than the rest. That
must have been a collapse in a rare earthquake, perhaps the last spasm of tectonic life
remaining in the ancient planet.

The thirty of them were to do what meteor-
ites and earthquakes had not been able to do.

Germyn touched the huge steel riser—merely touched it, wonderingly. The instant sequel
was a clanking of machinery from East and
West; two unregarded devices at the foot of
the slag pile which you might have taken for
abandoned junk stirred themselves. Their gears
groaned and elevated purple quartz eyes at
Germyn.

"Routine precaution," Tropile said precisely.
"They are First Alert against repair or trans-

port machines out of control. None of us must move at a greater speed than two miles per hour, or Second Alert will be activated, with hysteresis currents which would cause all our metal equipment to become red hot. Begin to apply your triton blocks."

Moving slowly, slowly, seven pregnant women and eight men crept down the slag pile, bent almost double under oxygen tanks, respirators and thirty pounds of explosive each. An eighth woman, Gala Tropile, followed them. Her burden was a huge coil of cord carried over her shoulder like a bandolier. The woven jacket of the stuff was laced into the pattern of a diamond-back rattlesnake, with good reason. They worked their way down the pairs of legs that supported the overhead. At each pair one paused, pulled a sticky one-pound block from its neighbors and smacked it against a leg. It stayed, and Gala Tropile passing by inserted an end of the rattlesnake cord into a drilled, sticky hole, leaving a yard of diamondback tail to trail on the cold ground. Slowly, slowly, they mined thus a quarter-mile of the overhead tube. Slowly returning, they all helped Gala Tropile knot the diamondback tails onto one unbroken length of the rattlesnake cord.

Meanwhile, slowly, the fifteen left at the riser had been circling it as if it were a maypole, winding it and winding it with more of the cord. Over the cord at last they placed things like wax seals, but eight inches across. They were shaped charges, queer weapons that did most damage where they were not. A shaped charge applied to a surface touches it along a circular line; most of the charge does not touch the surface at all. When it is fired it does no damage along the line of contact, but at the center of the circle it drills a neat, deep hole through almost anything.

There was only one casualty. An African applied a charge overcarefully and stepped back to admire his work; there was nothing to step back onto. He tumbled down the slagpile at more than two miles per hour. The moronic machines watching decided; Transport device out of control; apply Second Alert. Another of the nondescript machines littering the desolate plateau awakened, drained power from accumulators, and blasted out hysteresis currents toward the rolling human being. Before he reached the bottom of the slag pile his oxygen tanks glowed red hot and exploded, the metal burning brightly for a second. The rest of the mining party, on the fringes of the field, felt shoe-eyelets and zippers sear them, and their tanks on their shoulders were suddenly hot coals for an instant. The instant passed; the agony remained but grew no worse. Stolidly they continued their winding and pasting until the second party returned, paying out its rattlesnake cord.

Tropile was still tenuously mind-linked with the Snowflake through the green creature. He did not live the full life of the Snowflake, nor was he wholly out of it. It was the difference between coma and death—not too important to an observer, but the only thing in the world that matters to the patient.

There trickled into his comatose state a consciousness that the Pyramids had reformed their octagonal attack and were moving faster to grapple with the tread-mounted mystery before them. Rate of energy discharge increased; good, he noted. By now the lesser tasks of the eight subsidiary parties should be set up; his group was to trigger the detonations.

He led his thirty to the lee of a junked Solvay Process tower where they had cached their remaining weapons; the tail of the primacord fuse he embedded in a final yellow triton block fifty feet away. He steadied a rifle on a rusted plate and cracked a thirty-caliber mischmetal tracer bullet into the bright little target.

The block exploded and blew up the primacord, stuff that burned—exploded—at one thousand feet per second. The blast leaped to the riser first, and there was a rattlebang of shaped charges blowing their neat, white-hot holes around the fifty-foot pipe. It flared down the colonnade of spidery legs upholding the overhead tube, the explosions merging in a long roar, the flashes looking like a moving line of fire. Suddenly silence, and suddenly new, nonexplosive noises—creaks and grumbles of metal. The overhead tube sagged minutely in the center of its undercut quarter mile, sagged farther and crashed, split clean. Where it struck against a hundred jagged rocks or piles of rubble the cold and brittle metal broke in fragments, huge curved plates and shards. The shattering noise travelled through rock and metal to their feet and through their bones to their ears.

A wild gush of viscous liquid poured from the splintered butt-end of the overhead, and spurted like a hundred-pointed star from the perforations that encircled the riser. The unsupported curve at the top of the riser complained, sighed metallically and gave up the ghost. It leaned deeper and deeper, and the riser tore along its perforations; those white-hot holes had not only pierced but annealed the metal. Heated and cooled again, its crystalline structure had changed; now it could be drawn, and when it would draw no longer it would tear. Crashes again when the riser, greatest of trees, was felled. The top of it splintered, the annealed bottom of it yielded and slumped into a lazy figure-eight cross section.

It was happening also a mile to the South. Crouching behind the Solvay tower they saw lights on the horizon and felt in their teeth more distant crashes and screams of metal.

"We have done well," the Snowflake said to Tropile humorlessly. "We must now defend the breaches."

"Must we not?" the green person added sardonically on his own.

More of the quiescent machinery that littered the bleak planetscape stirred. From under a battery of dead, abandoned electrolysis cells crawled the primary food-main repair machines. They had not been in hiding. They were universal environment equipment; it did not matter where they waited until summoned by pressure drops in the main and the breaking of circuits built into the main's fabric. They had done their last job an earth-century ago, the meteorite-hole repairs to the riser. They had waited nearby since then and when the lead cells of a chlorine-factory complex wore out, the repair machines had suffered the cells to be dumped on them by disposal machinery. They could dig out on signal, and the signal had come.

There were about one hundred of them. They resembled hugely oversized tank-dozers to which had been fitted a variety of material-handling accessories: extensible cranes, pairs of hands, lift forks. They were not fighting machines, but by the nature of their mission they were built to survive natural damage and bull their way through to the injured mains against any conceivable opposition by earthquake, meteor, flood or lashing broken electric cable.

But not by man.

The thirty humans waited silently for the ten machines that ground toward the shattered riser and the fallen overhead tube: ninety other monsters angled across the gaunt planetscape towards the other enigmatic wounds reported to their deep-buried brains. With fascinated horror Roget Germyn unscrewed the lid from a box which bore an ancient stencil: ABERDEEN PROVING GROUND. Inside, in honeycomb cells, nested a dozen slim tubes with egg-bulges at one end and fins at the other.

"You will load for us as you were shown," Tropile said to Germyn. Tropile shouldered a bazooka, sighted along its barrel and caught the foremost of the repair machines in the cross-wires, three hundred yards away, coming fast.

The Snowflake died at that moment. In one burst of love, farewell and pain it transmitted through to Tropile the image of the searing blue line of plasmoid, the nutrient tank boiling dry, boiling them with it.

Germyn slapped him hesitantly on the shoulder—the signal for "armed and loaded." Glen Tropile collapsed under the trifling weight of the sheetmetal tube and missile and lay sobbing. He was dead; he had just died.

"Give me that damned thing," Gala Tropile said, wrenched the rocket launcher from him and shouldered it inexpertly.

"My God, be careful!" Germyn screamed. "They're atomics!"

"I know," she said shortly. She steadied the fore-end of the tube on a hummock, got her sight-picture, and put her finger on the button. A woman who had stood foolishly in line behind her and caught the rocket's exhaust blast clapped her hands to her burnt-away shoulder and collapsed, writhing. Nobody paid the slightest attention to her; their eyes were only for the little fireball that streaked into the leading repair machine and turned it into a big fireball. A red-purple mushroom cloud leaped into being above it, but before the cap formed Gala Tropile was snapping at Germyn: "Load! Load!"

That sector of the dark planet's equator was bright for the next hour with the death-throes of the hundred machines. Some men and women died with them. One box of the hot-wire rockets consisted of duds that had slipped through inspection down in Princeton. That group fought off the repair machines with rifle fire to pock and dimple their gears, and shaped charges hurled at a suicidal short range. Two were left of the thirty human beings in that group by the time their neighbors could turn their own rocket launchers to the flank.

18

After all was silent and the dead were numbered, the Pyramids came, gliding silently and slowly on their cushions of electrostatic force. They fitted themsleves into the black, cliff-high booths and waited . . .

They would wait thus until the end of time for food to absorb so they could go about their business of making more food to absorb, so they could . . .

The human beings, at first scared and angry and unable to turn their backs on the monsters, were at last surprised to find that they could pity the great dead stupid things.

19

If, a lifetime of labor later, one of those skinny and starving Ellis Island immigrants had returned, plump and secure, to his shtetl or Mediterranean fishing village, he would have been hopelessly out of place. No subways! No elevators! No all-night supermarkets! No friends, even, because the ones he had once known had changed so—or he had—that there was nothing to talk about. Such a person would have been an alien among his own people.

No more so than Glen Tropile, when he returned to life.

The naked, sweating, pugnacious members of the mouse pack tried at first to welcome him. He would have none of it. Not even from Gala Tropile—*especially* not from Gala Tropile, because the woman made the unforgivable mistake of throwing her arms around him. Sweat-stained, shaggy-haired, smelly—she was lucky her husband didn't throw up on her. He might have, if there had been anything in his stomach to void. That came later, when he realized that he would once again have to contend with the disgusting business of eating food, not to mention the even more disgusting business of getting rid of what the food turned into. (He mourned for the sweet, clean nutrient fluid of his tank—and its occupants, his more-than-siblings, his very self.)

Fortunately there was a war to be won. His task was to lead his army into battle.

But then that was done . . . and he was, tragically, still alive.

He closed himself off as best he could. His hands went often to the places at his temples where he had once been joined to the rest of the Snowflake. His eyes looked at infinity. He offered no speech, though he would answer questions:

Haendl: "How can we get back to Earth?"

Tropile: "The ship used for Sun kindling will be found at Latitude North 32.08, Longitude West 16.53. It will accommodate 114 persons and make the passage in six hours and forty-five minutes."

Innison: "How can we disconnect all our people from these damned machines? How do we wake them up?"

Tropile: "Neurosurgery machines used for disconnection of Components will be found against the North wall of the Reception and Reprocessing Complex and may be programmed manually to administer electro-shock through the forebrain which will have the effect of scrambling the pleasure-reflex you refer to by implication as 'sleep': after some hours of disorientation and mania the primary personality will assert itself. Notice should be taken that there will be a mortality rate of about seven per cent for this operation."

Germyn: "Can I get you anything, Citizen Tropile, for your comfort? Are you all right? Do you wish to see your wife?"

Tropile: "No. No. No."

The reclamation of the Components proceeded exponentially. At the start there was only the ragged tribe, reduced to two hundred by its war, tentatively recognizing a friend or a husband here and there wired into the network of the planet. With trepidation the neurosurgery machines, the first ones programmed by the hands of Tropile, were brought to the Components and they were awakened. Then there were a hundred and ten, and the ten had useful shadow-memories. They "guessed" that you worked this machine *so*—and that's the way it was. Then there were four hundred and ten, and the tribe was outnumbered and a little resentful of these well-fed come-latelies who had not been in the battle at all and who knew so much about this damned planet. Then there was a regular assembly line set up to process Components out, and the Sun ship, on a ferry run to return them to an astounded Earth.

Tropile was among those returned, sitting relaxed but unmoving, his eyes dead. He sat thus for three months before it occurred to somebody that "electro-shock through the fore-brain" might be what *he* needed.

It was.

Tropile was Tropile again, living, aching, looking up at masked faces.

Surgeons and nurses.

He blinked at them and said groggily: "Where am we?" And then he remembered.

He was back on Earth; he was merely human again.

Someone came bustling into the room and he knew without looking that it was Haendl. "We beat them, Tropile!" he cried. "No, cancel that. *You* beat them. Beautiful work, Tropile. Beautiful! You're a credit to the name of Wolf!"

The surgeons stirred uneasily, but apparently, Tropile thought, there had been changes, for they did no more than that.

Tropile touched his temples fretfully, and his fingers rested on gauze bandages. It was true. He was out of circuit. The long reach of his awareness was cut short at his skull; there was no more of the infinite sweep and grasp he had known as part of the Snowflake in the nutrient fluid.

"Too bad," he whispered hopelessly.

"What?" Haendl frowned. The nurse next to him whispered something and he nodded. "Oh, I see. You're still a little groggy, right? Well, that's not hard to understand."

"Yes," said Tropile, and closed his ears, though Haendl went on talking. After a while

Tropile pushed himself up and swung his legs over the side of the operating table. He was stark naked, and once that would have bothered him enormously; but now it didn't seem to matter.

"Find me some clothes, will you?" he asked. "I'm back. I might as well start getting used to it."

Glenn Tropile found that he was a returning hero, attracting a curious sort of worship wherever he went. It was not, he thought after careful analysis, *exactly* what he might have expected. For instance, a man who went out and killed a dragon in the old days, why, he was received with great gratitude and rejoicing, and if there was a prince's daughter around, he married her. Fair enough, after all. And Tropile had slain what was undoubtedly a foe more potent than any number of dragons.

But he tested the attention he received, and there was no gratitude in it. It was odd.

What it was like most of all, he thought, was the sort of attention a reigning baseball champion might get—in a country where cricket was the national game. He had done something which, everybody agreed, was an astonishing feat; but about which nobody seemed to care. Indeed, there was an area of accusation in some of the attention he got. Item, nearly ninety thousand erstwhile Components had now been brought back to ambient life, most of them with their families long dead, all of them a certain drain on the limited resources of the planet. And what was Glenn Tropile going to do about it? Item, the old distinctions between Citizen and Wolf no longer made too much sense now that so many Citizens fought shoulder to shoulder with Sons of the Wolf. But didn't Glenn Tropile think he had gone a little too far *there?* And item—well, looking pretty far ahead, of course, but still—Well, just what *was* Glenn Tropile going to do about providing a new sun for Earth, when the old one wore out and there would be no Pyramids to tend the fire?

He sought refuge with someone who would understand him. That, he was pleased to realize, was easy; he had come to know a few persons extremely well; loneliness, the tortured loneliness of his youth, was permanently behind him, *definitely*.

For example, he could seek out Haendl, who would understand everything very well.

Tropile did.

Haendl said: "It is a bit of a let-down, I suppose. Well, hell with it; that's life." He laughed grimly. "Now that we've got rid of the Pyramids," he said, "there's plenty of other work ahead. Man, we can breathe now! We can plan ahead! This planet has maundered along in its stupid rutted bogged-down course too many years already, eh? It's time we took over! And we'll be doing it, I promise you, Tropile. You know, Tropile—" he grinned—"I only regret one thing."

"What's that?" Tropile asked cautiously.

"All those beautiful bazooka fission bombs

we fired! Oh, I know you needed them. I'm not *blaming* you. But you can see what a lot of trouble it's going to be now, stocking up all over again—and there isn't much we can do about bringing order to this tired old world, is there, until we have the stuff to do it with again?"

Tropile left him much sooner than he had planned.

Citizen Germyn, then?

The man had fought well, if nothing else. Tropile went to find him and, for a moment at least, it was very good. Germyn said: "I've been doing a lot of thinking, Tropile. I'm glad you're here." He sent his wife for refreshments, and decorously she brought them in, waited for exactly one minute, and then absented herself.

Tropile burst into speech as soon as she left; he had been hard put to it to conform to the polite patterns while she lingered. He said: "I'm just now beginning to realize what has happened to the human race, Germyn. The false division into Sheep and Wolves. *You* fought like a Wolf . . ."

Tropile stopped, suddenly aware that he had lost his audience. Citizen Germyn was looking tepidly pained.

"What's the matter?" Tropile demanded harshly.

Citizen Germyn gave him the faint deprecatory Quirked Smile. "Wolves," he said, gazing off into the distance. "Really, Citizen Tropile. I know you thought you were a Wolf, but— Well, I told you I've been thinking a lot, and that's what I was thinking about. Truly, Citizen," he said earnestly, "you do yourself no good by pretending that you really thought you were Wolf. Clearly you were not; the rest of us might have been fooled, but certainly you couldn't fool yourself. Now, here's what I think you ought to do. When I found you were coming I asked several rather well known Citizens to come here later this evening. Oh, I explained everything to them very fully; there won't be any embarrassment. I only want you to talk to them and set the record straight, so that this terrible blemish will no longer be held against you. Times change, and perhaps a certain latitude is advisable now, but certainly you don't want—"

Tropile left Citizen Germyn much sooner than he had expected to also. So at last Glenn Tropile turned to the last person on his list who had known him well. Her name was Gala Tropile.

She had got thinner, he observed. They sat together quietly, and there was considerable awkwardness; but then he noticed that she was weeping. Comforting her ended awkwardness, and he found that he was talking:

"It was like being a god, Gala! I swear, there's no feeling like it. I mean, it's like— well, maybe if you'd just had a baby; and invented fire; and moved a mountain; and transmuted lead into gold . . . maybe if you'd done all of those things at once, then you might have some idea. But I was everywhere at once,

Gala, and I could do anything! I fought a whole world of Pyramids, do you realize that? Me! And now I come back to—"

He stopped her in time; it seemed she was about to weep again. He went on: "No, Gala, don't misunderstand, I don't hold anything against you. You were right to leave me. What did I have to offer you? Or myself, for that matter. And I don't know that I have anything now, but—"

He slammed his fist against the table.

"They talk about putting the earth back in its orbit!" he roared. "Why? And how? My God, Gala, we don't know *where* we are. Maybe we could tinker up the gadgets the Pyramids used and turn our course backward— but do you know what our orbit is supposed to look like? I don't. I never saw it.

"And neither did you or anyone else alive.

"It was like being a god—

"And they talk about going back to things as they were. Wolves! Citizens! Meditation, the cheapest of the cheap thrills! Flesh! Mere flesh! Mere flesh! Once I could see, Gala, but I'm blind now! I was a ring of fire that grew! Now I am only a man, now I will never be anything but a man unless—"

He stopped and looked at her, confused.

Gala Tropile met her husband's eyes. "Unless what, Glenn?"

He shrugged and looked away.

"Unless you go back, you mean." He turned to her; she nodded. "You want to go back," she said without stress. "You want to get back

into your tub of soup again, and float like a
baby. You don't want to *have* babies; you want
to be one."

"Gala," he said, "you don't understand. There
was a wonderful, wise old person, witty too,
who happened to be green and happened to
have tentacles and happened to be dead. I
wanted to know him better; his thoughts tasted
good. And we knew that there's a tri-symbiotic
race in the Magellanic Cloud beloved by all
that part of the Galaxy. You see, they have
learned a fact about—call it God. We wanted
to visit them. And the Coalsack Nebula isn't a
dust cloud at all; it's a hole in space. There are
races in the Universe whose entire cultural
history is the building of a slow understanding
of the nature of that hole. Think how the
thoughts of such a race would taste to an
eightmind—"

He stopped. "You think I'm crazy," he said.
"Crazy to forget that I'm an animal, that I can
never be anything but an animal, that a twitch
at the neck of a gland matters more than the
tri-symbiotes of the Magellanic and their Fact.
You may be right."

"What I think," whimpered his wife through
tears, "is that you'd be dead again."

Dead? Tropile was startled at the vastness
of the misunderstanding between them. Where
could one begin, to explain things to a person
who thought that when you had lost all your
physical attributes in the tank of a Snowflake
you were *dead*? He tried clumsy bribery:

"You know," he said, "if I went back, I

think I could take care of the Sun for you, and probably reverse the propulsion machinery."

The only answer was a wail.

Doggedly Tropile retraced his tracks. He rapped on the door of Citizen Germyn, and the man blinked at him. It was a moment before Tropile recognized the Quirked Smile. "Oh, am I doing something wrong?" Tropile asked. "Sorry. If it's because I didn't stay to see your freinds—" An ironic, deprecatory tilt of the head, meaning, Yes, it damn well is. "I just wanted to say something."

"Come in," said Citizen Germyn. "How nice that the moments just beore retiring should be made more interesting in this way." Meaning, It's pretty late for this, chum.

Dismayed, Tropile stayed in the doorway. "I'll make it quick, Germyn. What would you think if I went back to the binary planet? Had myself wired in, and all?"

There was a pause while Citizen Germyn gravely considered, his nostrils faintly expanded, as though sniffing the bouquet of an unfamiliar bloom. Then he smiled. The scent was, after all, beautiful. "I think that would be quite fine," he said warmly.

Meaning: How nice it will be not to see you any more.

Nor was Haendl less enthusiastic. Haendl was sound asleep when Tropile knocked. Bleary-eyed, he snarled, "Couldn't it wait?"

"Not this, I think," said Tropile steadily. He told the man what he was thinking of. The scowl on Haendl's face evaporated at once, replaced with a big smile. "Do it, man!" he boomed. "Hell, we'll build a statue to you!"

Meaning much the same.

Tropile turned away, alone in the silent town. It was late night now, and warm. Warm Autumn of the five-clock-year-cycle . . . the next of which he would himself initiate, by Re-Creating the Sun in person from— He grinned. From a tub of soup.

And would he find seven others to date it with him?

No. Not on this planet, he thought; it would be a lonely tub of soup. He would tend this planet's hearth fire for it better than the Pyramids ever had done, but alone he could not hope to be a ring of fire that grew. At least he could shed the flesh, be free of that tyranny. Standing in the street he looked up at the stars that swung in constellations too new and changeable to have names. *There* was the universe! Words were no good, there was no explaining things in words; naturally he couldn't make Gala or anyone else understand, for flesh couldn't grasp the realities of mind and spirit that were liberated from flesh. Babies! A home! And the whole grubby animal-business of eating and drinking and sleeping! How could anyone ask him to stay in the mire when the stars challenged overhead?

He walked slowly down the street, alone in the night, an apprentice godling renouncing mortality. There was nothing here for him, and therefore why this sense of loss?

Duty said (or was it Pride?): "Someone must give up the flesh to control Earth's orbit and weather—why not you?"

Flesh said (or was it his soul—whatever that was?): "But you will be *alone*."

He stopped, and for a moment he was poised between destiny and the dust. . . .

Until he became aware of footsteps behind him, running, and a voice: "Wait. Wait, Glenn! I want to go with you!"

And he turned and waited; but only for a moment; and then he went on, arm-in-arm with his wife.

And not—for ever and always again—not alone. There was one more. There would be others! The ring of fire would grow.

Announcing one hell of a shared universe!

OF COURSE IT'S A FANTASY . . . ISN'T IT?

Alexander the Great teams up with Julius Caesar and Achilles to refight the Trojan War—with Machiavelli as their intelligence officer and Cleopatra in charge of R&R . . . Yuri Andropov learns to Love the Bomb with the aid of The Blond Bombshell (she is the Devil's *very* private secretary) . . . Che Guevara Ups the Revolution with the help of Isaac Newton, Hemingway, and Confucius . . . And no less a bard than Homer records their adventures for posterity: of *course* it's a fantasy. It has to be, if you don't believe in Hell.

ALL YOU REALLY NEED IS FAITH . . .

But award-winning authors Gregory Benford, C. J. Cherryh, Janet Morris, and David Drake, co-creators of this multi-volume epic, insist that *Heroes in Hell* ® is something more. They say that all you really need is Faith, that if you accept the single postulate that Hell exists, your imagination will soar, taking you to a realm more magical and strangely satisfying than you would have believed possible.

COME TO HELL . . .

. . . where the battle of Good and Evil goes on apace in the most biased possible venue. There's no rougher, tougher place in the Known Universe of Discourse, and you *wouldn't* want to live there, but . . .

IT'S BRIGHT . . . FRESH . . . LIBERATING . . . AS HELL!

Co-created by some of the finest, most imaginative

talents writing today, *Heroes in Hell* ® offers a milieu more exciting than anything in American fiction since *A Connecticut Yankee in King Arthur's Court*. As bright and fresh a vision as any conceived by Borges, it's as accessible—and American—as apple pie.

EVERYONE WHO WAS ANYONE DOES IT

In fact, Janet Morris's Hell is so liberating to the imaginations of the authors involved that nearly a dozen major talents have vowed to join her for at least eight subsequent excursions to the Underworld, where—even as you read this—everyone who was anyone is meeting to hatch new plots, conquer new empires, and test the very limits of creation.

YOU'VE HEARD ABOUT IT—NOW GO THERE!

Join the finest writers, scientists, statesmen, strategists, and villains of history in Morris's Hell. The first volume, co-created by Janet Morris with C. J. Cherryh, Gregory Benford, and David Drake, will be on sale in March as the mass-market lead from Baen Books, and in April Baen will publish in hardcover the first *Heroes in Hell* spin-off novel, *The Gates of Hell*, by C. J. Cherryh and Janet Morris. We can promise you one Hell of a good time.

FOR A DOSE OF THAT OLD-TIME RELIGION (TO A MODERN BEAT), READ—